THE KINGFISHERS

KAREL NOVÝ

THE KINGFISHERS

Illustrated by Mirko Hanák

Translated by Peter Avis and Jiřina Tvarochová

 BROCKHAMPTON PRESS

First published in Great Britain 1967
Designed and printed in Czechoslovakia
by SNDK Children's Book Publishing House, Prague
for Brockhampton Press Limited, Leicester
Text copyright © 1963 Karel Nový
Illustrations copyright © 1963 Mirko Hanák
English translation copyright © 1967 Peter Avis and Jiřina
Tvarochová

Winter is leaving

Winter! Winter! All the time. Would it never end?

Two kingfishers, Or and his wife Kik, perched sadly on the alder and hazel boughs above the snow-covered, frozen river. They were hardy birds and did not feel the cold, but they were hungry. That is what winter meant for them, and often they were very hungry indeed.

When the sun shone through, it looked a sickly yellow, and when it set in the pink and scarlet sky, it promised a sharp frost at night.

'Away, nasty winter, go away,' Or used to cry.

At last the sun began to smile and grow warm. The snow crept away. And the kingfishers revived.

'It's coming at last,' said Kik.

Some siskins flew by, a whole crowd of them — they were inspecting the crown of a young pine — and the kingfishers sat nearby and listened to those busy birds telling one another that the larks were coming back, and that one of them had already been trilling away above a field close by.

And Or remembered how his father used to say — when Or was small — that in April the lark will trill, even if it's freezing still.

Winter was leaving. Spring was coming!

The snow slipped first from the southern hillsides. The bushes stretched their black branches as people often stretch after a good meal, and beneath the bushes, against the grey and yellow of the dead grass, tiny white flowers appeared, looking like the last traces of snow, and trembling for their young lives in the cold.

And there on the tip of an ancient spruce, a blackbird was tuning up like someone trying an instrument that had been put away for a long time. Yes, yes, it would be all right again, the blackbird with the yellow bill would whistle gaily again.

The snow was melting fast, but the northern slope, overgrown with a tangle of hornbeams, oaks and hazels, in which Or and Kik lived, seemed not to know that spring was coming. There the snow was still packed tight, held by a firm armour of ice which encased the stream in its airtight grip.

In the daytime the kingfishers usually perched on the stones among the black and rusty leaves of the uncovered southern hillside, or they peered out from the tree roots gnawed at by the water, and stared at their own stretch of the river. When would the sun with its warm beams bite through the ice at last and loosen it so that they could go hunting again?

They felt that the day was not far off when their stream would appear again, when its ripples would splash and glisten in the sunshine or the moonlight. All through that period of winter, while the river was frozen and hidden beneath the snow, they had seen the stream in their dreams, where it was perhaps even more beautiful than in reality.

No, that moment could not be far off when the ripples would appear again and go dashing and humming along.

But today, they still had to fly to a foreign territory, to the river of the kingfisher Lit. A ditch led from the river to a building full of clattering and spookish noises. It was a water-mill. There the ice had broken up and it was a good place to fish — but, of course, only if Lit was not lurking around, and there were no cats and dogs, or humans, about.

This winter had exhausted the kingfisher and his wife, who had been living below the village by the Black Rock for three years. How many times had beautiful Kik nearly fallen, tired with hunger, as she flew over Lit's territory. Her body felt so heavy! She could not carry it with her short wings. And when she landed there was no one in the whole world but Or, her husband, to help her and to bring her a fish, perhaps a dace or a roach, in his often blood-stained bill.

At last the ice cracked. At last! The large floes and small drifts groaned and creaked as they were carried away. The water roared down the old river bed, as if it wanted to make up for the immense silence which had smothered it for so long.

It stretched its loosened arms and embraced alders, beeches, boulders. It foamed. It flooded meadows, fields, roadways, and it even rushed up to the houses of the village.

All through the night Or and Kik listened in their old burrow below the Black Rock to the furious hissing and droning of the river. It all sounded like a song to them, fort his roar of wild power was a sure sign that the cruel winter was leaving and that spring was coming, bringing them the kind warmth of the sun and, together with it, enough food.

It must have been nearly morning when Or asked:

'Are you asleep, Kik?'

'No, Or,' she answered. 'I've been awake for a long time. I'm thinking of the spring to forget how hungry I am.'

Or nestled up to his wife and said:

'I think of beautiful things, too, when I want to forget my hunger. Just now I'm thinking of the way you'll glitter when the sun shines. No other kingfisher can have such a lovely wife as mine.'

It was a long time since Kik had smiled so happily.

They snuggled closer together and dreamed that spring was really here, that the banks were already green and full of sun and butterflies and dragonflies, and the meadows full of flowers and those shining beetles which were so tasty after a big meal of fish — but it was no use thinking of meals like that in winter.

When they flew out in the morning, they saw nothing that looked like their old familiar river. The valley was flooded and muddy, and the droning water was filled with lumps of wood and the blackness of bushes and trees. Among the pieces of ice, a chopping block floated and, beside it, a cradle and a dead cow. Crows hovered above the rolling, frothy surface of the swollen stream.

There was nothing here that the kingfishers had dreamed of all through the night, no sun, no warmth and, above all, no safety.

They perched close to the water, looking for food.

They were lucky. In the bush where the blue birds were waiting hidden, a pike, too big for them ever to have taken it alive, was caught with its white belly facing upwards. They plunged at it.

Or tried to seize the pike and carry it to their tunnel under the rock.

But it was too heavy. And so they began to gnaw at it with the hunger they had suffered for so long and with the passion that takes hold of their fishing breed like fire.

Suddenly, a wild whirr sounded above them. Like a stone, a sparrow-hawk fell into the bushes. They only just escaped. They flew, screeching with fear, and all the time the whirr of the rapacious bird's wings seemed to confuse them. They zigzagged like streaks of lightning, overtaking each other as they fled. They kept on flying, even when they knew that the enemy was no longer chasing them.

They found each other at home. They rested. Their hearts were still beating wildly, but they were already thinking of hunting again. They shuffled along the long tunnel from their nesting place out into the open. They thought once more of the spring, of the sun, of having plenty of food — and they thought of danger too.

They flew warily up and down their bank and only from time to time did they give out a warning, timid 'ts-ts'!

Once they noticed a small crowd of humans running excitedly along the edges of the flood water with rakes and crooks.

Only towards evening did the water begin to fall; the current grew calmer and no longer roared. In a few days it would subside completely; the river would be gentle and peaceful once more and above all clear, so clear that nearly everything on the bottom, shoals of big fish and swarms of little fish, would be seen — the kingfishers would only have to perch in the bushes above the shallow and wait.

The next morning the grass was strewn with dead fish cast there by the falling waters, and among them were a lot of dace and roach, beaten to death by the ice. Anyone who happened to turn up could choose what he wanted.

A rust-coloured fox flashed by beneath the Black Rock and in a moment he had disappeared again into the forest carrying a large fish.

The snows melted and the forest awoke; the ice went away and the river opened. A thrush competed with the blackbird in song.

It was still cloudy and cold winds whistled. Icy springs bubbled down the slope filling the empty gullies. But at midday the sun was already warm, its smile was reviving life in every bush and tree in the valley and throughout the Czech lands.

Spring is here!

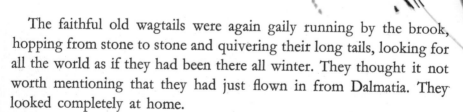

The faithful old wagtails were again gaily running by the brook, hopping from stone to stone and quivering their long tails, looking for all the world as if they had been there all winter. They thought it not worth mentioning that they had just flown in from Dalmatia. They looked completely at home.

But really, it was much braver to have lived through the winter in Czechoslovakia!

Crowds of siskins arrived and gathered on the hazels at the Black Rock. They discussed what to do. They cried out, fell silent, then cried out and argued again. In the end they agreed with one voice that it was time to break up. They bade one another farewell and flew off quickly in their pairs, to look for somewhere to nest.

Orioles called gaily and a chaffinch wandered from tree to tree, singing continuously:

'Spring is here, spring is here! Let's make merry!' He was overcome with joy.

Blackbirds sang, and a stock-dove grunted in the hollow of an old alder which had been carefully inspected and cleaned out by the green and black woodpeckers. Wrens chirped and titmice twittered; turtle-doves purred and robins spied out their hunting grounds, but far enough from the looking-out posts of the butcher-birds — those birds were not reliable neighbours!

The Black Rock reverberated as though it had strings and the wind was playing on them.

'Let's not delay building our nest,' said Or suddenly to his wife. Her ears might have blocked, and she did not hear. She looked up into the sun, ruffled her back, hopped up higher in the bush and, in a flash, she was gone.

Or, taken by surprise, looked in the direction in which Kik had flown.

What had happened? Why had she fled? Where had she gone? A moment later he hurried after her. Growing more disturbed, he flew up and down his territory and cried: 'Kik! Kik! Darling Kik!' What had come over her? Was she hiding for fun or was she fed up with him?

Tired out, he waited in the bushes. When would she come back?

After a short rest, he flew off again, calling out her name.

He seemed to hear her crying up in the forest. He dashed there. But there was no further sound, nothing to see. He flew into the territory of Lit, but he did not dare to draw too close to Lit's nest. He perched on a bush by a path and bemoaned his sudden loneliness.

And there a gentle tweet reached his ears.

'I'm here!'

Full of joy, he rushed after the voice. But at the same moment a blue bird flew away and glided swiftly down the stream. Or darted after it.

Kik zigzagged and disappeared again into the thicket.

Or forced his way through the bushes and came face to face with Lit.

'What can I do for you, sir?' Lit called out.

'I'm looking for my wife,' answered Or.

'Aren't you lying, sir? Isn't it perhaps *my* wife you are looking for? Or perhaps you think that you are in your own domain, and not in mine? Wasn't it enough when you stole my fish in the winter? Do you now want to rob me of my wife?'

While they argued, they heard a mocking female voice above them: 'Oh, oh! Why are you quarrelling, you two neighbours?'

The two kingfishers quickly looked up, but they could not distinguish through the net of greenish branches which Mrs Kingfisher it was. This upset them even more and they prepared to fight.

Suddenly a shot rang out nearby just above the river.

The two birds jumped apart in fright and flew off.

Or tried to reach his territory as fast as he could. He dashed in. And there, as if nothing had happened, sat Kik on a stone beneath a bush.

'Where have you been?' snapped Or.

She laughed.

And only now did Or remember that last year at just about this time the same thing had happened. Suddenly she had flown away and simply disappeared. And yes — of course — the year before last, too, and every year in the spring. She flew away for a time and later answered all Or's questions with a simple shrug of the wings.

She wanted to be alone, quite alone. She wanted to fly free and without a care, just as she used to when she was very young. Then she would fly like a streak of lightning down the brook and up again, to swim and sunbathe and ruffle her feathers. But what she used to like best of all was to look into the mirrors of the pools at her blue, red and yellow beauty.

The young kingfishers, dressed-up boys, used to pursue her whenever they saw her. And when she vanished they would call her in honeyed voices:

'Come, my beauty! Come, you sweet and lovely thing!' In the moonlight Kik had then dreamed of the new home she would build with the strongest and bravest of all the young heroes who were dazzled by her beauty. The most valiant of all had been Or. He had stuck to her like a shadow from the first time that he had seen her. She had managed to disappear. She had hidden in a bushy bank and had watched him flying desperately up and down and calling to her.

She had enjoyed this game of hide-and-seek. It had thrilled and excited her.

Would he find her? Or would he not? And, if he did find her, what would he say, that strange, beautiful youth?

For three days and three nights she had kept appearing before him and disappearing again.

Finally she had grown tired of this game. In the end she had been charmed by his persistence and devotion, and so she had shown herself to him, not wanting to leave him ever again.

'I believe,' Or had said then, looking at her with a bewitched expression, 'that you must have come to us from a land of paradise.'

Her face had shown no response, as though she had not heard the compliment. But, in fact, her heart had leapt at the kind tone of his voice.

'What is your name, my beauty?'

Blinking her eyes and overcome with embarrassment, she had answered: 'Kik.'

'That was the name of the mother of my ancestors,' Or had replied. 'The name is as old as the world, and only the daughters of those who remember that they used to live by the mouth of two large rivers in the far, far distant land of the first humans, can be called by that name. How noble the name is! For that, my beauty, I love you even more. I have seen you before. I saw you even before I met you. I saw you in my dreams. But you are even more beautiful in reality, Kik.'

That was their most starry night.

The next day they had begun to look for their own place to live, their land of promise.

'I'll leave the brook, and we'll move to the river where there is more food. I'll find you the best and safest bank a river can have,' Or had said boastfully.

'As you command,' Kik had answered humbly. He had flown ahead singing. She had followed him. Or had become her fate.

Every year Kik thought of those days of her courtship and wanted to be alone, disturbed by no one, so that at least in memory she might live through that time again.

How time passed! Kik and Or had brought up four nests since then.

Destruction

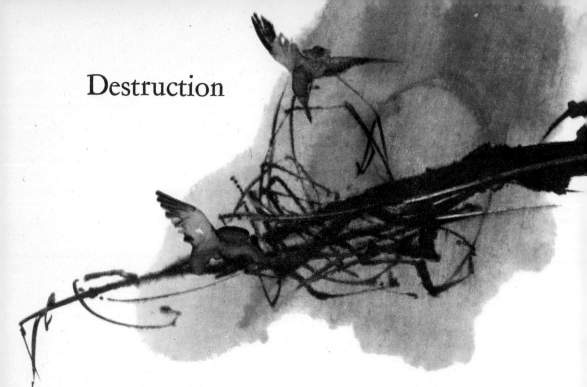

After the flood large patches of reddish and grey soil were left on the meadows and fields and tracks, for the river had scoured out a lot of sand and stones on its way down from the mountains. But already the water was getting cleaner. When the sun shone on it you could now see the bottom in many places. That was what the kingfishers liked, for they could then spot the fish, their prey.

'Now we can begin to build our nest,' said Kik. 'We could be idle before, but today the time has come for work.'

Yes, it was nearly time for nesting.

The kingfishers found a steep bank and began to dig out a tunnel. They worked as hard as they could to finish the job quickly, but it took several days to dig a passage through the hard clay.

Suddenly, during a break in their work, they heard a wagtail's call of alarm:

'Tizit! Tizit! Watch out! Watch out! Watch out! Danger!'

They listened tensely and heard other birds pass on the warning cry.

'Shall I go and see what's up?' asked Or

Kik lightly tossed her head:

'But what could happen to us here? I suppose some kite or buzzard's hanging about, but those fellows are no danger to us while we're working here in our tunnel. Why don't all the others do the same as us? Why do they want to build their nests in the branches or even on the bare ground?'

However, the danger turned out to be greater than anyone could have foreseen. It was neither a kite nor a buzzard that had appeared. They fly in and fly away again, although their visits usually mean that some small bird will die. The wagtail or his wife would come to grief if they did not spot the bird of prey in time. Yes, the kite and the buzzard fly in, fly away and life goes on. But this alarm grew louder all the time.

All the birds living at the Black Rock were screeching away when the kingfishers decided to come out of the half-darkness into the light. At last they too had heard the sound of human voices.

And now they saw a crowd of villagers, men with shovels and pickaxes on their shoulders, pulling carts behind them. The men began to spread along the riverside and a few of them made their way right to the kingfishers' own bank, to the place where, for four years, Or and Kik had lived a more or less peaceful life, hidden from the world, from birds and beasts of prey, from stray cats and dogs, even from humans.

All the feathered inhabitants of the Black Rock were on the branches screeching in alarm at the intruders.

'What do you want here? How dare you disturb us? Go away! This is our home, not yours!'

There were blackbirds and buntings, warblers and siskins, goldfinches and bullfinches, thrushes and wrens. Usually when these birds met they behaved like strangers, even pretending not to see one another. But in this hour of danger they were all of one mind. They all felt equals — each for all and all for each.

The kingfishers were not used to flying through the top branches. They kept to the undergrowth, below the screeching, clamouring flock. The flock fluttered to and fro. One moment it drew near to the humans and the next it darted off in fright. The wagtails behaved like heroes, running along the bank quite close to the men, swearing and screaming at them all the time:

'What do you want here? What do you mean by coming to scare us? Clear off!'

Possibly the men did not even notice the agitated screeching of the flock or the heroism of the wagtails. They got on with their job. They started banking up the river along the very stretch which was a boon for birds and animals but a bane for humans. The men had decided to imprison the free-flowing stream between raised, solid banks, so that it could not overflow and flood their homes, or cover their fields with mud and stones, killing their crops.

First they had to uproot the alders and hazels and dig ditches. At the same time they set to work hacking out the rock. The saws worked: shrr-vrr, shrr-vrr, and the pick-axes crunched: cr-ump, cr-ump.

The stone-breakers began to lay the rock bare while others set about felling the beeches which had been happily growing there.

The birds thought that the human work would be completed by nightfall, and that the men would disappear, satisfied with the destruction they had caused. They had done enough. It was a pitiful sight. Dead bodies of trees lay with their heads hanging down from the rock, and many had been sawn into logs. The men built a shed from the limbs of the fir trees they had felled and put their tools in it when they left.

The sun set. The birds grew calm again.

'But what about this?' asked the wagtail as he walked round the shed. 'Is it meant to be a trap for us? Don't anyone dare go inside!'

The kingfishers returned home. They circled for a long time above their hiding place where they had lived through so many seasons. The ground everywhere was beaten down, and polluted by the smell of humans! And one of the largest trees of the Black Rock, the ancient spruce, had been felled right by their home. Its sawn trunk stared at them in ghastly whiteness.

But surely all this would soon be grown over again with healing grass, and new trees would rise up!

The kingfishers comforted each other as well as they could. Comfort is what every frightened heart needs. But they still spent a troubled night. They were seized by the fear that the humans would return and complete their destruction.

Even before daybreak they set out along their river to feed and get up their strength for another day's work on their nest. But they were out of luck.

A mist wafted off the water and a crow was perched by the shallow where the kingfishers usually managed to surprise their prey.

She was strutting about like the lady of the manor and she called out proudly to Or who had come to perch not far away:

'Caw, caw! By claw and paw, don't you dare come here!'

Suddenly the wagtails appeared, having heard her call, and immediately they screamed:

'Tizit! Tizit! Beware of danger!'

The crow eyed them with contempt and treated them as if those little tail-wavers were not even worth pushing out of the way with her large, black beak.

'Tizit! Tizit! Away!' the wagtails cried, over and over again.

Or cried out too, and in a moment a host of ruffled-up creatures were gathered around. They all looked keen for a fight, cursing and circling ever nearer to the crow, their unwelcome visitor.

At first the crow was not put out at all. Then she was only pretending not to bother about what the riff-raff of forest and water were up to. Finally she could control herself no longer and she began to peck at the wagtail. He jumped nimbly aside and went up to her again, madly wagging his overgrown tail.

Carried away by his courage, nearly all the birds now closed in on the crow and were poised to attack. She grew uneasy, took wing and flew slowly away. She swore to have revenge, and above all on the wagtail for the disgrace she had suffered from him — that saucy bird, who now flew after her with his rushing swinging flight, mocking her as he went.

By now it was light and soon the men began to amble in to continue their work. All the anger and lamentations of the birds were in vain: the humans took no notice of them. Perhaps they did not even hear them.

Man is not a crow, my friends, whom you can simply chase away.

The first to leave the protesting flock were the stock-doves.

The kingfishers followed later. Their home was destroyed.

They flew off upset, knowing that now they had to look for a new place to live.

Flight
into the unknown

Or flew up high, Kik followed him. But she grew dizzy from the height and called to him to come down, or she would fall, she would crash and hurt herself.

Kingfishers are not accustomed to heights. They are always so busy fishing that they have forgotten how to climb to the clouds. Their flights are short. They carry themselves heavily and steer badly with short, blunt tails.

Or and Kik soon came down again just above the river and flew on. They rested frequently. Where the banks were overgrown, they landed. But wherever the couple stopped, other kingfishers were already living, and when they spotted Or and Kik they showed their hostility, screeching at them and driving them from their waters.

'This is our fishing ground, don't you trespass here, off with you!'

'We don't want anyone else's place, we're looking for our own,' Or and Kik politely replied.

They went to bed in the grass beneath a bush. The stream played below them. Above them the forest hillside was full of voices. They crouched, huddled together for warmth, and now Kik felt very sad, as people do when they have lost their home. She sobbed softly.

'Don't worry about it, Kik dear, sobbing doesn't help,' said Or, comforting her. 'Better think of how we're sure to find a territory even finer than the one we had at the Black Rock.'

'It's a bad thing not having a roof, being a stranger everywhere. Perhaps, Or, we should go back tomorrow. We'll never have such a good time anywhere else,' said Kik, still regretful.

'Remember,' replied her husband, 'how many times you were dissatisfied and envious of those who had better hunting grounds than you.'

'True enough. I was inexperienced. I was spoiled by good living. Let us go back there, Or. Perhaps the humans will have gone from the Black Rock by now and will leave us in peace.'

But Or shook his head:

'Where man has set foot once, there he will remain. And I don't feel like living on top of him, as man is our greatest enemy. My father used to tell me that, and so it must be true.'

'The Lits live quite near to his dwelling and nothing has happened to them yet,' protested Kik.

Or did not answer. He pricked up his ears. Beneath them, on the sandy bank, a crouching shadow seemed to be passing in deathly silence. Or tensed his whole body, waiting.

'What do you see?' Kik breathed out excitedly.

'Quiet,' whispered Or.

It was a dark night and the sky was covered with heavy clouds spitting rain from time to time.

Now they were all eyes and ears, but noticing nothing, they grew calm again. They felt very sleepy already. They were also rather tired from flying and from hanging about strange pools poaching for food.

Living off others is nothing to be proud of!
They had experienced enough of the shame
of this in the winter that had just passed. Need
had driven them to it. But then, everyone has to
do what he can to keep alive.

No sooner had the kingfishers begun to fall asleep
than the heart-rending cry of an attacked animal rang out.
A second later, before they could recover from their shock,
two heavy bodies were tumbling around the bush, locked together
in a single mass.

Was it a fox that had seized a hare?

In the darkness beneath the frightened birds, some terrible combat
had broken out. The sand crunched and there was a thunder of lashing
legs and tossing bodies. The kingfishers sensed rather than saw the
life-and-death battle between the two animals. They pressed to each
other in alarm. They felt their blood grow cold as horror gripped
them.

Hardened though they were by their fights with fish and small
enemies, they became petrified when they heard the terrible
noises of these animals, which seemed so enormous
in the black darkness.

The water splashed. The combatants had
rolled down into the river, but even there
the battle continued unabated.

And now the kingfishers fled. They flew
up and away. Away from that terrible place!

They flew above the murmuring river.
Every now and then they spotted the water
when a star broke through the clouds.

They flew side by side.

'Watch out!' called Or. 'I think
the river bends here.'

'All right,' answered Kik. 'Don't
worry, I'll stick to you. But how
far have we still to go?'

'Keep going for a little while.

Maybe I'll find a good place soon.'

'Oh, if only the moon would shine! If only the stars would shine!' sighed Kik.

Was it real, or were they dreaming? Was it a storm they heard, or perhaps a roaring flood?

As they flew on, the noise drew nearer, the steady roar grew louder and then it was as if someone had torn them apart with a mighty blow. Or was sinking, losing his senses.

He caught the sound of his wife calling. He reached up after it and immediately got back his breath:

'An owl!' he cried in terror. 'Kik, drop to the bank!'

But his call of anguish was swallowed up in the roaring noise just beneath them.

'Kik! Kik! Where are you?'

Kik had disappeared and Or dashed to and fro, trying to cry above the roar of the weir which had appeared below just as they had been pounced upon by the eagle-owl.

Supposing the hunter of the night had caught and torn her to pieces?

Or flew higher, and immediately dropped down again calling all the time. Now he seemed to see two eyes glowing yellow and coming towards him at a tremendous speed. He folded his wings and fell like a stone. Then, just above the water, thundering, frothing and spurting, he began to flap his wings again. He rushed here and there and hurtled straight into the darkness, without thought, without sense. He felt death behind him.

Then he hit his bill and head against a tree or a rock and lost consciousness.

When he opened his eyes again it was broad daylight.

His bill ached and his head throbbed!

The cruel memory of the night flashed through his mind. Was it true that Kik had disappeared? And where was he himself?

He stood up. But he collapsed immediately. A thought ran through his aching brain and caught on it like a talon.

'Perhaps I'm dying!'

Blood was flowing from his bill. He leaned on a wing and stood like a beggar leaning on his staff.

Where was he?

In a cranny of a strange house near the weir which never stopped roaring. And in the house there seemed to be someone who was pounding and clacking all the time.

The house was a mill.

Or ruffled up when he realized that he was within the reach of human hands. He called out plaintively:

'Ts! Ts!'

From somewhere below his wife's voice answered:

'Or, Or! Where are you?'

'Here, Kik, my dear!'

The sheeny blue of Kik's wings flashed before him. Kik flew up to him and, if they had had arms like humans, the two birds would surely have hugged each other.

'What happened to you, my love?' asked Kik. 'And where were you?'

'An eagle-owl chased me. I cried out. I thought you were flying with me.'

'I couldn't hear anything for the roar of the weir. I was looking for you and then I hit this wall in the darkness.'

'There's blood pouring from you,' said Kik, terrified. Only now did she notice his blood-stained bill.

Or took hold of himself and tried to smile:

'That's nothing,' he said. 'It aches a little, but the pain will go. What's important is that we have found each other again and that nothing has happened to my wings.'

Kik was silent for a while, as she gazed lovingly at her husband.

Then she said: 'I was weeping all through the night. Without you, Or, I just couldn't live.'

Or threw out his chest.

The joy of meeting again drove away his pain and Kik's love made him feel strong.

'What now?' he asked. 'Where shall we fly to? I think we've both had enough of wandering.'

'Certainly,' she answered. 'But our luck's held out in spite of everything, hasn't it?'

'Yes,' he sighed with relief. And after a moment: 'Let me just have a little rest now.'

At that moment a sparrow flew in and perched on an alder before the gable of the mill where the kingfishers had settled. When he spotted them his eyes popped out with surprise. Then he cried out:

'Chirrup, chirrup! You won't cheer up here, my friends!'

And he disappeared immediately. But a moment later he was back again with a crowd of his companions, who began to be very unpleasant. They mocked and sneered at Kik and Or, and when the kingfishers tried to ignore them, they flew at the cranny and cried out:

'Get off, you riff-raff, we're not going to put up with any tramps like you settling in our mill!'

'Off, off, or we'll peck you to death!'

'Who would want to live here,' Kik called out at them angrily, 'in such a noise?'

Or paid no attention to the sparrows, as if they were not worth it. 'Let's go,' he said.

They spread their wings and disappeared, leaving the chorus of enraged sparrows behind them.

As soon as they reached the water's edge Or was able to wash and cool his head, and everything was all right. Well, nearly all right. For he still felt quite a pain from his crash against the wall, although he kept it from his wife. He had a strong will.

In search of a home

They were no longer flying above the river. Only after a while did they notice this. Behind them, behind tangled clumps of alder and willow, sallow and young spruce, the weir continued to roar, but now they had beneath them the quiet, smooth, clean water of a brook.

Or and Kik flew slowly up the stream.

Kik managed to catch a fat roach. They both tucked into it as if they had not eaten since the winter.

When they had finished eating they rested among the roots of an old alder.

'Are you all right now?' Kik asked Or.

'Yes, quite. But something seems to be worrying you all the time, dear.'

'I can't forget our old home,' Kik answered.

'Let us only hope that we're near a new fishing ground now,' said her husband. 'If you ask me, we wouldn't do badly to stay here.'

No sooner had Or finished speaking than there was an agitated whirr right in front of them, as a sturdy kingfisher fluttered his wings above the pool.

So even this place, this quiet pool, was already occupied!

There was nothing to do but to fly on. As soon as they took off, the owner of the domain spotted them and tried to catch them up.

As Or had not properly recovered yet, he was easily outpaced.

'You just try poaching here, you tramp,' the old resident called out angrily at Or. 'Get back where you came from!'

Or answered quite gently:

'I would get back if I could. I used to have a better hunting ground than yours, but some humans took possession of it. Now I can only look for a new one. I'm not a poacher, I'm just an honest fisher bird who has fallen upon bad times. You, too, may meet the same fate. I would not wish it upon you, nor upon any of us. But bad times are no respecter of kingfishers. I fly on with my wife when we see that a territory is occupied. We are flying on now, so leave us alone.'

'Indeed, you're a friendlier fellow than I'd thought,' said the old resident, speaking now quite gently. 'Well, I'll allow you to do a bit of fishing, but then be off with you immediately. I've had unfortunate experiences with tramps, they've already attacked me several times and tried to get me out of here. I can't trust anyone, and our own breed least of all.'

'What a pity,' commented Or, 'that we kingfishers are so intolerant of one another. If only we would stick together like the sparrows, for instance . . .'

'Don't tell me these stories, tell them to the others, not to me when I've had such terrible experiences with my fellow beings. Just fly away as quickly as you can.'

'Yes, you're as obstinate as the rest. And that's no virtue, but only makes you stupid.'

'Perhaps you're right, but it's more likely that you want to insult me, so be off with you,' the holder of the fishing ground cried out angrily as he lunged at Or.

But Kik, who had been following the discussion from a close distance and busily watching the enemy's movements, put out her wing to parry a heavy blow of the bill aimed at Or's chest. The old resident flew up in anger, but did not dare to launch another attack against the pair.

And so, without further trouble, Or and Kik flew on again up the stream.

As they went on, the valley grew narrower and more thickly forested. But from bend to bend, as far as they flew, the hunting grounds were already divided up, with their owners watching jealously over their territories.

They reached a bend where an old mill stood, and they stopped and thought of sheltering there for the night.

The sun hung above the ridge of the forest, already about to set.

'I feel lonely, so lonely,' sobbed Kik.

'I understand. But complaining won't help. In my opinion, the best thing would be to spend the night inside the mill. After all, wasn't it a mill which saved us both? You just wait here for me and I'll look round for a good place.'

Kik agreed, but she asked Or to wait while she looked, as he was obviously more exhausted than she was. Or reluctantly let her go. The mill was quite small. It sat beneath the pine forest like an old man, with the thatched roofs of the stable and barn looking grey and matted with age.

Kik quickly flew round the building. Her heart began to beat a little faster. The noise and commotion inside the mill scared her. The antiquated machinery grinding monotonously reminded her of the distant roll of the weir. She could find no suitable place to shelter and was about to leave when she noticed that the water flowing into the mill flowed out again the other side, quiet and clean. This attracted her attention. She had always been a curious creature, as women are. And so she got under the wall where the water was streaming out and into a dark room where a wheel was turning. She could hardly see anything for the darkness. A patch of light showed at a small window and Kik dashed out and flew to Or.

'I've found a place for the night,' she called, as she approached.

And indeed, the birds spent a good night on a beam in the wheel-house, and the following day Or felt quite better.

'Ts-ts,' he called, 'it's not as dreadful in a man's house as I'd imagined.'

They flew up to the small window and looked down below. There they spotted a three-coloured cat. She sleeked silently along the ditch, sat for a moment, and stole on again, spying carefully as she went. She caught sight of the kingfishers, gave them a sweet smile and put on an innocent air.

In their secluded life the kingfishers had rarely seen a cat and now they looked on this one with surprise.

'Miaow, miaow,' she said, gently blinking her eyes, 'how beautiful you are, little blue birds. Fly to me and let me caress you.'

At that moment, a chaffinch settled on a bush above the cat and let out a piercing cry:

'Murderer! Murderer! Murderer!'

And so the kingfishers left the mill without delay.

They set out again up the stream. They had not flown far when they came across a wide expanse of water. On one side stood a spruce forest, on the other spread a green meadow, with another forest behind it.

'This is where I should like to live, I like it here,' exclaimed Kik. 'What a beautiful fishing ground! But surely someone is living here already.'

'Yes, life is difficult for fisher birds these days,' replied Or, 'every place is occupied. Can it have been like that in our fathers' times?'

'It was probably just the same,' laughed Kik.

As she spoke, a pair of mallard settled on the middle of the water. There was a great splash and the waves spread out, corrugating the surface of the pool.

There could have been no better proof of the seclusion of this forest pool than the arrival of these big shy birds. They had apparently just returned from a far country where it was so warm that the water never froze. 'It's interesting,' Or reflected, 'that ducks leave us alone while kingfishers can't stand one another.'

Kik gave a loving look at the water, rippled by the ducks' vigorous paddling.

And Or said:

'I can see you have fallen in love with this place. So let us stay here.'

'But supposing someone's living here already?'

'This pool could well support three families,' said Or. 'Now let's have a proper meal and then we can begin to look for a good place for our home.'

'But if someone . . .'

'If someone arrives and he won't listen to sensible arguments then we shall put our strength to the test. I have a right to life and to a home and family just as much as anyone else.'

'Oh!' sighed Kik. 'You can't imagine how I'm looking forward to settling down in peace and quiet. I only wish I were sitting on a nest of eggs right now.'

Or let out a cry of joy and flew back and forth across the water, shining bright and blue. He returned to Kik and they flew together to the shallow where they managed to catch their fill of small fish.

Then Or looked for a suitable place to build a nest.

He found it on a steep hillside beside a gigantic grey boulder beneath clumps of alders, raspberries and blackberries.

'What do you think of this place, Kik? I don't want to decide without you. I think it will do. And this boulder here will mark where we live. We shall be able to find our way home even in the dark and it will protect our entrance, too.'

Kik agreed eagerly and Or set straight to work. He dug into the hard ground with his bill. He still felt a pain from the blow he had received, but he did not let it worry him at all. He went on digging without stopping, pounding at the earth like a pickaxe. Soon he had disappeared. The only sound was the dull thud of his bill and the only thing to be seen was the soil flying out of the passage.

Kik pushed herself into the tunnel behind Or and helped him to carry out the soft, loose soil.

Whenever they felt like a meal they stopped working and flew to the shallow. Not many birds were hunting there and they found many more fish to catch than at the Black Rock.

Within a week the passage had been dug out and they had only to think of the final extension and the hollow for their nest.

They were tired after working so hard, but happy knowing that their wandering had come to an end and that they had found a new fishing ground and a new home.

An enemy
flies in

In the morning they woke fresh and happy, and flew straight to the shallow. The water was so clean that they could see to the bottom everywhere.

'Good morning,' a wagtail called to them, from a rock in the middle of the pool. 'I don't know you yet, but I say good morning because I'm polite, as a wagtail should be. Are you by any chance thinking of settling down here?'

'We've settled already,' said Or. 'And we're glad that someone of your tribe is here, and that it's you, such a kind bird, as I can see, who is to be our neighbour.'

'I'm not so kind to everyone,' the wagtail answered. He added: 'I've been living behind this alder for two years. And how do you come to be here?'

'We lost our home, we had to leave and wander the world like tramps,' said Kik. 'You can't imagine what a dreadful time we've had and what we've been through.'

'This is a good place to live. You won't find better than this pool anywhere. Of course, kingfishers have lived here before. I'm surprised they moved away. I wonder if they met with some misfortune? I haven't had time to ask Mrs Titmouse yet if she's had any news of them. I mustn't forget to look her up and when I see you again I'll let you know what she says. Until then, take care of yourselves.'

The wagtail flew off, but soon he was back again to give them a warning: 'Oh, there's an eagle-owl living in the forest not far from here. Watch out for him!'

This was useful advice. To the kingfishers it meant: keep close to the bank and, if you cross the pool, fly zigzag.

'I'm thinking he might take you away from me,' Kik sighed anxiously.

Or smiled and said:

'Just take care of yourself and don't worry about me. After all, weren't there birds of prey living at our old place, too?'

'But none lived so near.'

The passage leading to their new home was quite long. They would be even safer here than in their old home because they had come up against a rock in the ground and been forced to dig the passage crooked.

Now they had only to widen the end of the passage to make their nesting chamber. Here, later, there would be a little heap of fish bones spat out by the kingfishers. When all was ready Kik laid her first egg. She sighed and cheeped a little, and then felt happy and proud.

That happened a week after their arrival.

Meanwhile the wagtail had told them the story of the kingfisher who had been living there until the year before. He had died in the winter, fishing under the ice, and not long ago his wife had moved away. She might well come back with her new husband, because this mill-pond, known as the Blue Pool, was one of the richest fishing grounds all along the brook.

'I can't let anyone else come here,' said Or, puffing himself up with importance.

He had already forgotten that, only a few days earlier, he had declared that this hunting ground could easily support three families. But then, of course, sudden good fortune often puffs a fellow up, making him silly and selfish.

As it turned out, the previous Mrs Kingfisher did not return. Kik laid six eggs. The effort strained her a little, and she grew thin, but it did not damp her spirits. Quite the opposite.

'It's time for me to sit on the eggs now, Or dear,' she said. 'I'm sorry for you, having to take on the hard work of feeding me, but if I carried on hunting now, I'm afraid the eggs would grow cold.'

'Don't worry,' said Or. 'I've been able to feed you every time since we met and now I'll feed you all the easier here at the Blue Pool. You know me, I haven't changed, it's my duty and I'm happy to do it. In any case, aren't we supposed to be dividing the work? You do one thing, I do the other. Your job is to lay eggs, and sitting on them is more important and valuable than my hunting.'

'No, hunting is just as important as sitting on eggs. Without your hunting I could never hatch any eggs, and we wouldn't have any young ones.'

All around, the quiet, blue mill-pond rang with bird song. The air seemed to tremble with birds' voices, beads of sound dropping from the sky and the branches to the peaceful surface of the Blue Pool.

Many bushes were already in blossom. Alders and silver birches and forest hardwood trees quickly broke into leaf. And how good the grass smelt!

By now most of the mother birds were sitting on their eggs, but there were still some late-comers who had only begun to look for down and moss, and the stalks of last year's grass, to build their nests.

The wood-pigeons cooed and the turtle-doves purred.

Suddenly a cry: 'Cuckoo! Cuckoo!'

An echo replied, and at that moment a grey bird crossed the pool.

The birds fell silent as if they had heard a shot.

The wagtail flew to the rock in the middle of the pool and called out: 'Watch out! Watch out! Danger!'

They all froze still, crouching close to the arms and bodies of the trees.

Mother birds sitting on their eggs and nestlings hardly breathed as they anxiously pressed their dearest treasures beneath them.

Father Great Tit, who had lived for years in the old alder at the edge of the pool, slipped like lightning into his hole and chuckled to have such a safe retreat from the enemy hovering and prowling outside.

'Don't push so much. You'll break the shells if you're not careful,' Kik whispered excitedly. It was only her second day sitting on her eggs, and she took great pride in the task.

Only that big pair, the drake and his wife, kept calm and went on fishing.

Mrs Duck had found a snail and dragged it to the shallows where she was trying to open it. She had quite a job to peck through the hard shell of the tightly-packed snail.

The drake stood by, giving advice. In return he wanted a morsel of the delicacy, but his wife was angry and said she needed no advice.

She hurried up the bank into the ferns and gulped the prize herself.

'Watch out! Watch out! Danger!' the wagtail still called out, although the large grey bird was no longer to be seen around the pool. The menace had vanished.

The birds sang merrily again. Once more they began looking for beetles, larvae and caterpillars, catching flies, and chatting.

Or wandered contentedly along the bank of his hunting ground. A dragonfly flashed above the water and suddenly Or was swooping after it. The dragonfly fled towards the bank. It darted aside and dodged Or, who shot past like an arrow. He hardly had time to flap his wings and avoid hitting a tree trunk.

The kingfisher had wanted to take the dragonfly to his Kik — but decided not to. Once he had failed he was not going to bother any more. But he felt sorry all the same, as dragonflies are a great delicacy for kingfishers.

He sat perched on a branch of an old willow leaning over the water and there he waited. Something stirred close by: just look at that! The wren's little home.

Curious, Or poked his bill into the hole and heard a tiny voice:

'I wish you good day, Or! I am Mother Thumb. But please don't look in here — I wouldn't like anyone to know where we live.'

'Don't worry, I shan't eat you,' growled Or. 'I have enough fish and beetles, and that's all I care about.'

'No hard feelings, Or,' trilled the wren, 'but you know how every mother gets worried about her children.'

'Tizit! Tizit!' the wagtail warned again.

Or, who had wanted to tell Mother Thumb about the bravery of the inhabitants of the Blue Pool, quickly huddled closer to the wren's grey nest hidden among the roots and was silent. He crouched down so that the blue of his plumage blended with the green of the leaves.

And from this hideout he saw the grey bird again. It was sitting as cool as a cucumber in the grass on the opposite bank and looking at the wagtail.

What had taken its fancy here? It surely wouldn't dare to stay.

Oh, what a blow that would be!

But the wagtail was not a bird of timid thoughts. He cried out:

'Friends! Friends! After it, after it, after the terror! Don't be frightened. Let's all swoop on it together and we'll give it what for with our beaks! Pluck up courage, friends! Quick, quick! We'll show it we're not a lot of cowards at the Blue Pool to be played around with as it likes. Into battle, into battle! Away with it!'

And Mrs Wagtail came flying to join Mr Wagtail on the rock. Even though this was her second day of sitting on her nest, she stood beside her husband and cried out with him.

The grey bird seemed to be biding its time, waiting to see what would happen. It seemed to be wondering — would they take up the fight or not?

'Look, look,' cried the wagtail at the top of his voice, 'it doesn't even dare to fight us two! Quick, friends! Into battle! For the defence of the Blue Pool!'

But the Blue Pool was as silent as if all bird life there had died out except for two wagtails.

At that moment, Mr Wren joined them. He cockily lifted his little tail and began to mobilize the other birds.

Mother Thumb, hearing him, moaned away in her nest: 'Oh dear, if my husband loses his life, what will become of me then?'

'If even the tiniest of us is not afraid,' said Or, 'it would be shameful for me to stand back.'

And so he flew up and gave a piercing call:

'Everyone, everyone, after the raider!'

His rousing call worked. In a moment, nearly all the birds, most of them carried away by the example of the wren, started up with a tremendous noise against the intruder. Wives now left their posts and took to the field with their husbands crying: 'Hurrah! Hurrah!

And even Mother Thumb was among them.

If my husband dies for the safety and freedom of the Blue Pool, then let me die, too, she thought to herself.

With combined strength, the small birds swooped down upon the grey giant which now seemed to be growing frightened. It flew a short distance away.

They pursued it all the more furiously: 'Kill it! All for each and each for all!'

The enemy was driven off for the second time. And then they drove it off for the third time, chasing after it up the brook.

The most frenzied in the chase were the wagtails.

Suddenly, the grey bird disappeared into the forest on the other side. The birds were very relieved and they rejoiced, forgetting their hunger, their duty to sit on their eggs, and everything else. Full of enthusiasm, they discussed the details of the battle.

'I gave it a fright! I would have poked its eye out if it hadn't dodged me,' boasted Mr Thumb.

The smallest bird boasted the most and gave the others a big laugh. But all agreed that he was the most courageous — even the smallest heart is capable of great heroism.

Kik slept through this combat for the safety of the families living at the Blue Pool. The noises of war had not penetrated into the dark depths in which her nest was buried. And so she was surprised when Or woke her and told her how the victorious battle had gone. She was overjoyed that the enemy had been driven off and that Or was safe.

When Mr and Mrs Wagtail returned to their nest and the good mother bird sat again on her eggs, it seemed to her that there were more of them than before, and that one was unusually large.

And so she quickly hopped off the eggs and examined them carefully. Yes, one was a real monster! How had it got into the nest?

'What's wrong? What can you see there?' Mr Wagtail asked anxiously.

'I can see that — one egg is an odd one!' she answered with alarm.

'You certainly are beginning to see things,' said Mr Wagtail. 'Sit quiet, I'll soon relieve you.' And off he flew.

On the third day the cuckoo call was
heard nearby again, and once more the
grey bird appeared.

This time it was on the opposite
side of the Blue Pool, on the trunk
of an alder in which the great titmouse
and his family lived. The birds, now
emboldened, needed little urging. They
chased after the suspicious invader
all over again.

Yes, the grey bird was a cuckoo.
Once again she had lured the birds
from the Blue Pool so as to get back
there quickly before her pursuers and
lay an egg unnoticed in someone
else's nest, this time in the nest of
the titmouse.

Earlier she had even managed to
lay one in the home of the watchful
wagtail.

While the tiny inhabitants of the
Blue Pool rejoiced at their victory,
the cuckoo was quietly chuckling at
having been able to entrust her
future children to such orderly and
conscientious parents.

A turtle-dove flew in, laughing
and chuckling.

'Go away! Fly off!' the wren
screeched angrily. 'Don't you give
us a fright, too!'

Quiet steps

The inhabitants of the Blue Pool wanted only peace and quiet now. They had to attend to their nests and their families. They had food enough: caterpillars, beetles, greenflies, earthworms and tender herbs.

And the kingfisher, when he had lived at the Black Rock, never had such a rich fishing ground as he had here. Nor had Kik ever been so easy to feed at nesting time as this year. Besides young fishes and multitudes of roach and dace and gudgeon, there were also baby crayfish and masses of little snails.

All Or had to do was to perch by a sandbank or on a root sticking out of the water, and wait. Then he would fall like a stone upon his prey, rarely missing his aim.

Kik sat on her eggs almost all the time. Always before she had grown thin, but this time she grew fat from all the food supplied by Or. Of course, she often had aches in her chest and tummy, and then she would leave the nest and go for a flip. How big and beautiful the trees, the water and the stones poking through the surface of the brook, all seemed to her! How magnificent was the glitter of the spring sun, and how sweet was the sound of the water in the life-giving brook!

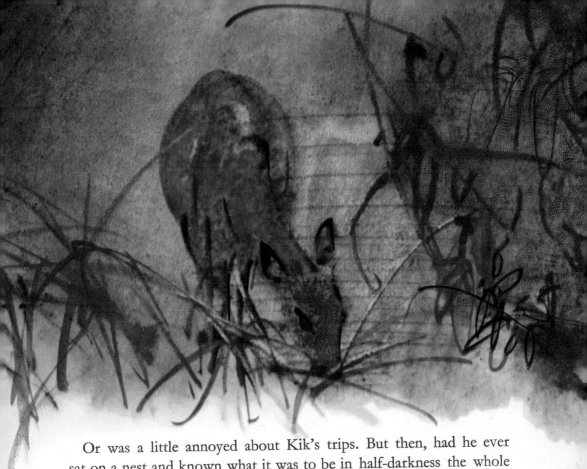

Or was a little annoyed about Kik's trips. But then, had he ever
sat on a nest and known what it was to be in half-darkness the whole
time and to have six hard pebbles for a bed? Of course, he had the right
to be anxious that no egg should get cold and that the germ of life
inside should be properly warmed, and should grow. But Kik was not
neglecting her duty. She knew full well what she could allow herself.

She would take only short flips, just to stretch her limbs and stir
up her blood, before hurrying straight home.

The first spring storm to strike the Blue Pool was wild and furious.
Before it broke, a sultry day hung above the forest and all the birds
felt that it would not end well. They flitted about anxiously, hardly
speaking a word, hardly uttering a note. They greeted one another
with barely a nod of the head. Towards evening, the thunder began
to echo in the distance, and the wind rose and grew stronger, rippling
the surface of the water and swaying the branches.

Rain began to fall from clouds which had quickly blown up. It
grew dark. Then the clouds passed over and it seemed that the storm
would blow itself out somewhere far away.

But soon came a roll of thunder nearby, and the sky was as dark almost as night. A fiery knife cut through the twilight while the thunder made the earth tremble and, in the midst of it all, streaks of lightning flashed quickly one after another.

The storm kept leaving the Blue Pool, then coming back, as if it wanted to destroy the place. It was nearly morning before it died down, but the drizzle continued.

The kingfishers were all right, for they spent the foul weather in the dry. But the other birds at the Blue Pool, the wagtails, warblers, chaffinches, siskins, robins, buntings, all living in the meadow by the forest, and the goldfinches, serins, turtle-doves and jays — they went through hell, with the mother birds sitting out the storm in their nests.

Father birds hid where they could, in rock crevices, hollows of trees, or under stones, while their wives faced the gale and the downpour to protect their eggs and nestlings. They did not sleep a wink the whole night. And by morning the drenched nestlings were shivering and cheeping with cold.

Not all the brave mothers managed to save their homes. Many eggs were thrown out by the wind, many nestlings fell out on to the ground and were killed, or if their nests were above the brook they dropped into the wild current and who knows where the turbulent waters carried the drowned creatures? Morning at the Blue Pool was gloomy, like the morning after a funeral.

The black woodpecker, the nuthatch, the stock-dove and the titmouse escaped calamity. Storms were no threat to them, unless lightning struck the hollow trees in which they lived. There they were as safe as the kingfishers in their tunnel. But how the others had suffered.

Mother Thumb also had her troubles. The wrens' little house was protected against the storm — but the water was rising and had nearly reached them. If it rose any more it would soak their nest and tear it away.

And Or was sad, too, as he could not see the fish in the muddy water. However long he stood at his perch above the shallows — which had become deep after the deluge — he could catch nothing. He had to start looking for beetles and flies. But the flies and dragonflies were probably drenched, too, and would be drying themselves in the bushes and would not come out. Or and Kik went hungry that day.

The sadness of the time did not spare even them.

It was a murky, chilly day.

But, strangely enough, the next day, right from the start, the sun smiled and the birds sang once more. Birds have very short memories. They hardly remember what happened yesterday.

'What has passed, what has perished,' — they seem to say — 'you will not bring back with even the longest sorrow. You will call no one back to life with even the deepest grief.'

A golden day blazed again above the pool.

Everything was nearly the same as before the storm. Life went on, all hurry and scurry.

Even the wrens' nest, which had been in such danger, had already dried out. All the battered nests were repaired within three days, indeed, soon you would never have thought that a force of destruction had passed this way.

Kik exclaimed: 'I can already hear my first baby knocking, I can hear its young life beating beneath me. How I am looking forward to it! Oh, how I am looking forward to my children, Or!'

Or's face was serious. He knew what was in store for him: twice as much hunting for food. If fish would do, that would be fine. But young ones need such delicacies as beetles, damsel-flies and dragonflies, as their tender throats cannot cope with sharp-boned, lumpy fish.

And yet he, too, was looking forward to hearing his children cheep. After all, the difficulties would not last for ever. Time would pass and the young ones would learn to fend for themselves.

He was just standing by the entrance to his passage and was about to fly off when he caught the sound of stealthy, tiny steps.

He drew back quickly. From his hiding-place, he saw on the narrow path below, a slender little animal in a clean red fur coat walking along silently — and Or could not help pushing out his head in curiosity.

The little animal stopped, looked around cautiously, sniffed the air and continued on his journey. Suddenly, some scent stopped him in his tracks. He looked here and there to trace it and saw the fisher bird's head above.

The slinky red creature was a weasel, the most treacherous enemy moving on the ground. For he does not hunt only by day, like the goshawk or buzzard, but by night, too, and he can squeeze into any-thing. You can never be safe from him anywhere, unless you live in a tree.

The kingfisher's heart was chilled with horror: supposing the weasel should try to clamber up from below or dig down to the kingfishers from above?

Once the weasel had spotted him it was no use retreating, and so Or let out a cry and flew out to see the direction the treacherous animal would take. But in fact the weasel grew frightened of Or and with a few leaps disappeared into the forest undergrowth.

Or saw him no more. Yet he was still filled with anxiety. He flitted in alarm from place to place, never settling. Every so often he was back in his nest with Kik or circling the entrance of his home.

He said nothing to Kik. He could not upset her now. After all, she was excited enough by hearing the tapping of the young ones beneath her.

Now she heard the second and third tiny lives under her tummy.

'If only they would break out of their white prison,' she wished.

That day she did not move away even for a moment, although she could not feel either her throat or her legs or wings — they might not have been part of her. Her whole body belonged to the nest. Only her thoughts did she have to herself.

Or's hunting was not very successful. But anyway, Kik did not touch even the few roaches he brought, while he ate hardly anything himself.

'The enemy is lurking, the enemy is lurking,' Or repeated to himself.

But the weasel seemed to have been swallowed up by the earth and so, towards evening, Or began to comfort himself that the danger was gone. The weasel might have been just passing by and when he had seen that the kingfisher was ready to fight he had moved off to his own territory.

Night was coming with a big, white moon. The warblers loved its pale beauty. When it appeared they perched on the branches above their nests and sang sweetly to the females sitting on their eggs.

Beside Kik, Or slept soundly, as his day's work had completely worn him out.

But Kik only dozed, tossing about like a cork on the water. She caught the sound of steps, quiet, light, cautious steps.

When the sound came nearer she awoke Or.

'What's up?' he asked drowsily. 'What's up?' He could not rouse himself.

'I can hear steps!' whispered Kik, and Or immediately gathered his senses.

It's the red-coated enemy! he thought to himself.

He ran quickly to the entrance.

The moonlight shone round the bend in the passage.

No one had got in then!

Or stopped at the very end of the passage and listened.

It was true! Steps! Very near, just behind the boulder by the entrance!

Or stiffened, his heart filled with fear, but with courage, too.

Suddenly, he heard something leap, but when he dared to look out into the moonlight it was no cunning enemy that he beheld, but a large, beautiful doe.

She stood there quietly, listening to see if the sound had disturbed anyone. She noticed nothing suspicious, so she bent her graceful neck to drink. She kept stopping, raising her head, listening, and when she was sure there was no danger she drank again.

Not a breeze whispered, not a twig stirred.

The big moon of a peaceful, spring night reigned over the pool, changing it into blue and silver, giving it the magic beauty of a fairy-tale.

Only the sound of the blackbird's whistle or the warbler's song broke the deep peace of that beautiful night.

Full of quiet content, Or returned to his nest.

'Sleep, my good Kik, nothing's the matter. A doe came here to drink. Does, they are perhaps the most innocent animals in the world,' said Or. 'I have never heard of a doe harming anyone.'

Family

At last relief came to Kik: her first baby got rid of its shell and cuddled up beneath her crop, tiny, thin and delicate. And then the second pecked its way out, and the third, too. After a day and a night, five fragile little creatures were trembling and cheeping as softly as a breeze through the first leaves of spring.

Or carried out the shells, flying with them far from the nest. He took them to different places so that no one who might find them could tell where the kingfisher's home was and discover them. It was always right to be cautious in these matters.

But the sixth egg would not awake. There was no tapping from inside. Only after three days did life begin to sound and then the parents were already busy looking for food for five hungry sons and daughters.

In three days the nestlings had become much stronger, growing in the warmth beneath their mother's body, and they could already make themselves heard begging for food.

'Don't cry so! Be silent!' their mother rebuked them.
But she might as well have said nothing — the little ones could not understand yet, and just cried on and on.

Or hunted food for the whole nest without a break. What a job: fish for Kik, flies and dragonflies for the young ones. And slugs and caterpillars, beetles and little tiny fish, too.

'How is the last one?' he asked anxiously whenever he came home with a catch.

'I'm afraid he won't come to life,' his wife replied.

But in the end even the last one came to life with the help of Mother Kik. But he was very weak, that little bird, and his strong, sturdy brothers and sisters bullied him, taking his food which their father never stopped supplying.

The mother, of course, watched with special care over the youngest and weakest one, and would not allow his brothers and sisters to do him any harm.

Every time the father came home he cast a dark shadow down the passage. Then he would assure them that it was him, Or, and no intruder. Or had long since arranged with Kik a signal so that they could safely recognize each other. Now the young ones, too, had begun to understand the signal and they were very happy whenever they heard it.

And they heard it frequently.

It was similar to our human speech, with questions and answers.

'Who's there?' asked Mother.

'Me, Or,' announced Father.

A week passed. It was one of the most difficult of Or's life, full of hunting and searching. But now it would be easier as Kik would begin to fly out, too, once her young ones had grown a little stronger.

A week means a lot in the development of a baby bird.

The young ones were already beginning to see. But it was hardly of any use to them yet. Only a little light reached them from what seemed like a reflection in the distance. The nestlings could merely distinguish the outlines of their mother's body and their father's head.

They were already beginning to grow feathers, too, but, of course, the feathers were still enclosed within stiff cases which looked like tough bristles. Their big heads were heavy and clumsy, and the fledglings could not yet hold them up. But in a short time they had learned to do so and they could understand what their mother was saying, too.

'Now, you are big enough not to be afraid of staying in the nest alone,' she told them. 'I must help your father to find you food. Your appetites are growing all the time, you need more and more and your father can hardly manage to feed us all by himself.'

'No! No! No!' they cried. 'Don't leave us, Mummy, we'll be frightened here alone.'

'What is there to be frightened of, silly children? No one knows about you, except your father, and Auntie Titmouse, and Uncle Thumb — and you've already outgrown him anyway.'

They had no idea what Auntie Titmouse or Uncle Thumb looked like. They took it for granted that they must look like their mother. Of course, they could not even imagine what an uncle or an aunt was, they had no picture of anything yet.

'When you grow up, you will catch fish, too,' said Kik. 'You will perch above the shallows and wait for your prey.'

These words they hardly understood.

They imagined, the silly little children, that their mother would for ever be sitting on them warming them, and that their father would for ever be bringing them tasty food for their hungry little bills. They thought that life would always be as it was now.

And so when Kik told them that she was going to leave them alone, they were surprised and frightened out of their wits.

'No! No! No!' they cried. 'Don't leave us! We feel so good beneath you, but when you leave, it will be so cold and the ground is so hard.'

'I'll warm you if you grow cold. But you must begin to warm yourselves, too. Get yourselves into a heap, but, children, mind you don't hurt the little one.'

And she disappeared.

If the children had been restless beneath Kik, talking whenever they were not sleeping, now they grew silent and pressed one against another, anxiously awaiting the return of their father and mother.

Father was back in a moment and the young ones welcomed him excitedly.

'Quiet! Quiet!' he called as he began to distribute dragonflies stripped of their wings. 'Quiet, or someone will hear you!'

'But our mother told us that nobody knows about us,' argued the eldest.

'Nobody? What is that?' asked the youngest.

'When you are older,' said their father, 'you will come to know everything. Now be quiet.'

If Kik had plenty to say for herself, Or did not want to waste any words now that he had so many things to worry about. And off he went again.

After a while the entrance grew dark again and Mother arrived. There was terrific excitement. Each shouted louder than the next:

'Mother, me! Give me! Me, me!'

She gave the largest piece to the smallest one, as he was her favourite.

'We're cold, Mother, stay here, stay here!' they cried.

'You must get used to it,' their mother told them. 'Quiet, quiet, hush!' But the young ones would not be silent. 'Shut up, I want to hear if someone is coming. Your father may be there.'

The entrance grew dark for a moment and then the light came in again.

'Quiet, youngsters, or I'll pull your tails,' snapped Kik, losing her temper, and at last the chicks did grow quiet.

Something pushed itself into the entrance again. Was it Or?

'Who's there?' asked Kik. There was no reply. Then it was not Or. Kik grew alarmed. Who could it be?

The enemy! The enemy! she thought. She dashed out through the darkness, her feathers standing on end and her bill stretched out like a sword.

She could distinguish nothing in the darkness.

But there was no doubt that something had sneaked in to rob the nest and that the young ones were in deadly danger. Her heart beat with terror, although she did not worry about herself at all.

'Who's there?' she called out again.

Silence. No one answered.

No answer is also an answer.

The silence was a challenge to battle, and Kik would not hesitate to fight.

She waved her bill.

She struck nothing.

So she hopped forward and jabbed her sword again into the darkness.

Something hissed at her so violently that it dazed her.

'Robber!' cried Kik as she dealt the enemy a powerful blow with her strong, sharp bill. She fought the unseen intruder and was ready to live or die, as she pushed herself forward. If she was to die, then let her family's enemy die, too.

'Run away or I'll kill you!' she cried as she kept battering with her bill, striking like lightning and without mercy.

The sound of hissing had been growing stronger all the time, but now it receded before the wild attack of the infuriated Kik.

The intruder who had sneaked in was the red weasel. He had come to rob the nest, bursting into the tunnel when Or was not at home to make a meal of his children. He had not expected to meet with any resistance, to have to fight and, on top of it, be defeated. Kik pushed the weasel back to the entrance of the tunnel. There the robber slid down the clayey hillside and crept, blood-stained, from the battle ground.

Kik let out a cry of triumph.

Or dashed home in horror, just in time to see the weasel hurry away and vanish in the undergrowth where he had disappeared before.

'Kik Kik! Kik!' called Or, trembling with fury and anxiety. 'Oh, you're bleeding! You've been attacked. Poor Kik, what has happened to you?'

She hardly had the strength to reply after her triumphant cry:

'I drove away the robber, he would have murdered our children.'

Or sat beside Kik, overjoyed to have such a brave wife. He felt proud that the mother of his children could not be daunted even by the most cunning enemy.

'Go to your children,' he said, 'go and have a rest. From today I know better than ever before what I must do: guard my home day and night. The weasel doesn't like to leave defeated, he'll be thinking of revenge.

But let him just try and steal into our home again, and he'll have two of us to fight!'

While Kik had been fighting with the enemy, the young ones had been trembling with terror. They had heard their mother's cries and the strange hissing, the hissing of something that had wanted to get in and kill them.

They shuddered in silence.

When their mother returned with their father, too, they felt like leaving the nest and romping about. But their wings, still so weak and thin, moved heavily. They cheeped loudly and what is more — they had forgotten their hunger!

'Did you hear your mother fighting, children?' asked Or after a while.

'We did,' they replied.

'Well,' began Or in a serious voice, 'your mother was hurt for you. Remember that. Remember that any one of you who is a coward will not be worthy of his mother and father.'

A few days after this battle another excitement took hold of the Blue Pool — a gigantic bird with an overgrown bill and overgrown red legs flew across.

It was early in the morning, and the feathered inhabitants of the Blue Pool were just setting out to hunt, when a pair of large, white wings drummed and stirred the air above the pool.

Mr Thumb cried out in terror.

For the first time in his life he was looking at a stork.

The wagtail made a threatening noise, but immediately grew silent again, for there was no danger. He had met old Father Stork in the years before he had moved to the Blue Pool and he knew that the stork did no harm to birds, and that he was mostly interested in frogs.

The stork flew several times back and forth across the pool, but did not stay, as he probably saw that there was very little food for him there.

He went and settled on the meadow by the mill.

The lapwing who lived there in the grass circled above him, uttering a cry of annoyance, but the stork did not bother, standing there calmly on one leg. He obviously had something on his mind.

The wagtails flew up and asked him many times what he wanted, but he did not glance at them any more than he had at the lapwing. He pretended that he neither saw nor heard them.

When the wagtails reported all this back at the pool, the chaffinches, who had met the storks too, said that storks were like that, hardly ever talking with strangers. They said also that they were very proud birds because they lived with humans, on the gables and chimneys of their houses, and in the high trees in their gardens.

'Perhaps that is where their pride comes from,' agreed the wagtail, nodding his head.

The stork stood in the meadow for a long time and reflected.

What about?

How can we know, when he spoke to no one? Perhaps it was not so important as his look suggested. Some humans also look as if they were thinking about something significant, and instead they may not be thinking of anything at all. And others again do not put on any look, but they are thinking just the same, perhaps about the everyday matters of food and shelter.

The stork stood for a long time in the miller's meadow.

Then he slowly flapped his wings, gave out a cry and with a great effort raised himself off the ground.

He flew away just as he had flown in.

'Humans say,' Mrs Chaffinch informed Mr Yellowhammer who was nesting there by the wayside, 'that he brings them children. Ha Ha! What a joke!'

Kik happened to be around and caught these words.

'Is that what they say?' she laughed with Mrs Chaffinch.

'Surely every mother, and that must go for human mothers, too, carries her baby, before she brings it into the world, beneath her heart.'

'Yes, yes, yes,' said Mrs Chaffinch, nodding her head. Her eyes sparkled gaily as she spoke. 'And that is why every mother loves her children with all her heart.'

Adventure

During the day Or searched for food with his wife. At night she stayed with her children while he guarded the entrance to the nest. He would be half asleep, half awake. He heard every whisper in the grass, every step of an animal coming to the pool to drink and quench its thirst after grazing.

Every day before dawn a doe appeared at the Blue Pool. She had her own path by which she came and returned, never straying from it on the way.

Or always enjoyed watching her sheeny back, and her beautiful, shrewd head with such large eyes.

How careful the doe was! When the wind blew and stirred the branches she turned round many times before bending down to the water.

And now along the path she had trodden, the hares, those furry bundles, were running too, frightened by the slightest rustle and movement of a branch, by the slightest whisper of sound. What a fright they got if a lizard appeared! They would immediately flee, and return later, making a wary detour to the pool. And what a shock when a squirrel suddenly jumped down in front of them!

Night passed so slowly that it seemed to be standing still above the forest, hesitating to leave. Sometimes it was dressed in black, more often its coat was blue and sprinkled with stars.

Before day came, there in the distance, far beyond the forest, the cockerels began to crow in unison, then the thrushes and blackbirds broke into song.

Soon Mrs Titmouse and her husband flew out from the heart of the alder, the wagtail cried out across the pool. Uncle Thumb the wren flew to the rock in the middle of the brook, a pigeon cooed, a jay screeched, a golden oriole called out as he flew by, the turtle-doves awoke and purred and the sound of the cuckoo echoed from the forest.

Little fish jumped above the surface of the water.

Kik awoke and slipped down the passage.

'Good morning, Or!'

'Good morning, Kik!'

'I forgot to tell you yesterday,' said Kik, 'that the wagtails have had a great big child born to them. Very big and very hungry — what bad luck for them. They're terribly upset, they can never feed it enough.'

'Why don't they feed it our way?' suggested Or.

'It's difficult to tell them that when they can't, Or dear. You should have realized that a long time ago.'

Or made a face as if his wife had insulted him. And he flew straight off.

The kingfishers' young were growing bigger and stronger every day. They made a lot of noise every time their parents brought them food. In vain did their mother and father tell them off and try to calm them down. The youngest was catching up well with his elder brothers and sisters because his mother favoured him most, not because she did not like her children equally, but because the weakest needed the greatest care. And yet, on the other hand, think what you will, Kik was most fond of the weakest. She tried to deny this to herself, but it was true.

Above the mill-pond the day blossomed and smiled. The air was full of the whistling and melodies of the birds, full of their bustle and the

humming of their wings. And on the green bank old thrushes and blackbirds were hopping about with their hordes of brown and black children.

There they went, as proud as Punch, taking their families out.

'See what we've brought up! They're still silly and clumsy, our little sons and daughters, but soon we'll teach them to be clever. And to fly. Little ones, show what you can do already. Don't be afraid! Well, how long are you going to take!'

And the children showed how they could rise into the air. What a beautiful feeling it is to be able just to fly and fly!

Of course, they did not know much about that yet. They were falling into the bushes, on to the grass, staggering about, and their heads were swimming when they finally landed.

But wisdom comes from experience. Everyone has to start from the beginning. Even the oldest bird at the Blue Pool had to learn the simplest movement when he was young.

Kik rather envied the parents of the young thrushes and blackbirds. However, she pretended not to see them. Mothers often seem, simply out of love for their children, to be narrow-minded and ridiculous. They take for granted that their own children are the most beautiful, the best brought up. And if they do praise other children, it is often only to have their own extolled in return.

'Oh dear, how are we to feed those children?' wailed Mrs Wagtail, jumping on to a stone. 'We have such an odd child. We can never give him enough.'

'Throw him out, throw him out!' twittered the chaffinch.

'Easy to say, easy to say! But didn't we hatch them all in the same way? And isn't he our child, too? He's starving, he's starving, we can't feed him enough, my heart is breaking for him!'

'And Mrs Tit in the alder has an odd child, too,' sang Mrs Chaffinch. 'Not I, not I! Only those who leave their nests. Not I, not I!' she added as she flew away.

The days, though they seemed to be long, flowed past as quickly as the water in the brook.

The young kingfishers' feathers were already bursting their cases and beginning to unfold. The birds were becoming restless. Curiosity to know how the world looked drove them out from their hard bed of bones. In vain did Kik give them a gentle telling off. And in vain did Or preach at them.

They pushed down the passage, towards the light, towards the mysterious light. And the most curious was the eldest.

'You'll fall if you venture too far,' his mother reproached him. 'You'll fall and we shan't be able to get you back to the nest. An enemy will find you and eat you up! A terrible rainstorm will come and beat you to death!'

It seemed to Or that there was no longer any danger of the weasel returning. And so once again he slept by his nest, by his children, after a tiring day hunting prey. As the young ones grew and became greedier and greedier, there was more and more work to do. But for the curiosity of his children Or would have fallen asleep as soon as he arrived home in the evening. However, the youngsters would not let him sleep, but begged him to talk and tell them something about the world, which was still beyond their understanding.

Their father would tell them how he himself had been a child, small and weak. He was the fourth to be born in a succession of brothers and sisters. And then again he would talk about how he had gained his experience after becoming independent, when his parents had told him that he had to earn his own living, to go out alone into the world. Once a human had nearly shot him, another time a dog had chased him.

'What's that, a human?' the children asked.

'He's a creature who does not fly and only walks on two legs,' said Or. 'He's so big, so big! And instead of wings he has hands which he can use to do everything. He can carry away whole forests, he can carry away rocks, he can even destroy from a great distance anyone he chooses!'

These were words that the little kingfishers only half understood. For what was that, a forest? What was that, a rock? What was that, a distance?

'We thought the biggest things in the world were us,' they said to their father, who only smiled.

'You'll see many things when the time comes for us to take you out. You'll see many things to surprise you,' he said, already falling asleep.

Kik was sleeping like a log beside him.

'Whenever will the time come? I want it to come tomorrow,' wished the eldest. And first thing in the morning, when his parents had flown from the nest, he crawled out of bed and went down the passage, down and down. It seemed to him endless.

Suddenly he appeared at the end and the full light of day dazzled him. He quickly closed his eyes and then opened them again. No, he could not look. The light hurt him so much! He did not know what was happening to him. He would rather have gone back into the gloom, into the darkness, but he stood frozen to the ground, petrified.

He heard an odd sound beneath him. A crackling and then a strange language.

'What good luck — a baby bird, a young kingfisher,' called a boy who had come here this Sunday morning from the village or the nearby mill. 'Come here and let's have a look at you.'

'Let him be, you'll frighten him,' replied a second voice, much softer and sweeter.

'I only want to look at him,' the first voice insisted.

The eldest of Or's children naturally understood nothing, feeling only that someone had taken him from the place where he had been standing dazed by the sunlight.

At that moment he caught the sound of his father's cry of anguish: 'My boy! My boy!'

And immediately after he heard, too, the pained voice of his mother: 'Oh, terrible! They're taking my child! Oh! Wretched me!'

'Defend yourself,' the father called out to his son.

And the young one obeyed, beginning to beat his bill against the human palm. But the boy held him tighter, so that the fledgling could not move at all.

'Let him go, poor little thing,' said the girl who had come along with the boy. 'See how frightened the old ones are, flying about and screaming. Don't torment them so.'

'What do you mean?' answered the boy. 'I only want to bring the little fellow up. I'll take him home, he won't have a bad time, I'll feed him well.'

'No, never. I won't let you,' the girl cried angrily.

The boy smiled.

'He'll have feathers as blue as your eyes, Rosie. His blue feathers will be like a dream of far-off places.'

'Yes, if you leave him in his nest and sometimes see him flying up and down the brook. But how can you talk about far-off places if you lock him up in a cage? Let him go, poor thing! Look how heavily he's breathing, his heart must be beating like a hammer.'

'I won't let him go,' said the boy.

'I'm not talking to you any more,' said the girl in a fierce and sad voice. 'I shall get angry with you and never be friends with you again because you are so cruel.'

'I won't let him go because the silly little bird would fall on to the ground and hurt himself,' said the boy, laughing. 'I must put him back in his burrow. I only caught him for that. And I only held him for so long because I wanted to see your good heart, Rosie, and make the little bird learn that the world is full of danger for him and that he must be well prepared to face it. Look how frightened his parents are! I expect they told him not to leave the nest.'

'So put him back then, the poor little thing has had quite enough of a lesson,' said the girl gently. And the boy stepped up to the boulder and released the fledgling in the passage. It immediately disappeared inside.

The boy and the girl smiled happily at each other, took each other by the hand and left by the narrow path along the side of the pool. Or and Kik at once stopped crying.

'I thought until now,' Or said to Kik, 'that humans were our greatest enemies. But perhaps that is not always true. There's probably a difference between them. I expect they're like us, good and bad.'

'Poor child, poor child!' Kik sobbed all the time. She had not yet recovered from the shock.

The presence of the boy and girl had upset Or and excited all the other birds of the Blue Pool, too.

For months no one else had passed this way. The mill was quite a distance from here and the miller came only as far as the mill-dam. A narrow path led round the pool behind the meadow where the lapwing lived. Once hobos, those gay mill spirits, always out of work, would sometimes follow this path. They would get food and lodging in the mill before wandering again along the brooks and rivers, on and on.

Of course Or did not know this, as he had not been living here then. But Auntie Titmouse talked about it. She had still been a little girl then. How time passes! Yes, Mrs Titmouse talked about it, she liked to talk, and she liked to mock the other birds for the silly things they did. But now she had done a silly thing herself because, as we know, she had allowed a cuckoo's egg to be laid in her nest.

'What do those humans want here? Why did they come here?' whimpered the stock-dove. 'Do they think they're going to make a habit of it? Oh, nasty humans, once they stole my young ones. I saw them carrying them off in a bundle. My heart bled so much. They were beautiful children, a son and a daughter. They carried them away, God knows what they did with them.'

'And once they destroyed my eggs,' said Mr Thumb the wren. 'I used to live in an orchard by the mill. Such a splendid nest I had. But no,' the little bird suddenly remembered, 'I would do man an injustice. It was his four-legged servant, his slave dog. He sniffed us out, drove us off and ate the eggs. No, no, man didn't harm us, but he did my father.'

'We were driven from our old home by humans,' said Or. 'That I can never forgive.'

'But they didn't hurt your little son, they nursed him and put him back again. I saw it, I saw it,' the wagtail called. 'They looked into my nest, too. They found it easily enough, but they didn't hurt a feather of any of us. I'm not afraid of anyone, not even a goshawk, not even a man,' said the wagtail, puffing himself up.

But there was no time to chat any more. At home hungry throats were waiting and cheeping.

Or's eldest son had been taught his lesson. He shrank back in the nest from his father and mother.

But wisely his parents were satisfied with the punishment he had received from man by being caught and enclosed in the palm of a hand. After all, hadn't he been scared to death, too, imagining, poor thing, that man would crush him to pieces?

Shots

'It won't be long now before we take you out,' Father Or said to his youngsters.

'Only your wings and tail feathers must grow a little more still,' added Mother Kik.

'Surely we're big enough already,' they pleaded.

'Patience, patience!' said their mother, soothing them. 'Learn it because it is the most beautiful quality kingfishers have. An impatient bird won't catch even a fly. You have to wait for everything, and most of all you have to wait to fly from the nest.'

Still the youngest went on:

'But we're so curious to see what it's like outside in the daylight. What a tree looks like, and water, and how the fish swim and the dragonflies fly.'

'Well, let young Or tell you,' laughed their mother, glad now to make use of her eldest son's experience in controlling her children.

But in spite of all the instructions and all the scolding, the children pushed down the passage towards the light.

Light! Light! It seemed to be ringing as it infiltrated into their nest. It enticed them, attracted them, awoke a strange thirst in their hearts, it drew them out from the darkness into the world, out, out, out!

'How beautiful it must be outside,' said the children as one after another they crowded and squeezed their way towards the light, getting nearer and nearer to it all the time.

Or realized that nothing would hold them back any longer.

'Look, children, I see the time has come for you. These are beautiful days full of sun and you are now big and strong enough to look at the world in which you are to live and hunt in good times and bad, just as they come. Let's go out. But you must be careful and obedient and respect every signal. You must take notice of every word. The world is full of enemies and you know almost nothing about them yet. You must keep together close to us. We shall show you how to fly, how to steer, and when you have learned this we shall show you how to hunt. But before you go out into the light, you will be given names to know who is who.'

The father spoke more seriously than they had ever heard him before and the children kept as silent as the sleeping wind.

Yes, it was a serious moment. Everyone experiences childhood in his own way and looks forward to his first step into life, while at the same time being afraid of it. But in any case, it is a step you have to take!

Night was falling on the pool in darkening circles and with it came a great silence. The birds grew quiet and went to sleep.

But Mr and Mrs Wagtail were still seeking food for their enormous, hungry young cuckoo and the titmice, too, were looking for something to satisfy their unmannerly child in the hollow of the alder.

Both the cuckoo children were growing at a furious pace and trampling on the wagtails' and the tits' own young. While the other birds were falling asleep, content at having the day's work behind them, the cuckoos' foster-parents, themselves hungry, were still flying about, searching for larvae, caterpillars, beetles, anything they could find.

The kingfishers were up, too.

They were spending a happy evening giving names to their children. Or had brought a big roach for the celebration and everybody ate to his heart's content. The parents thought up short, sharp-sounding names.

By right, the eldest son was called Or after his father, and the eldest daughter Kik after her mother. Then the next son was called Roon after his grandfather, and the youngest, his mother's favourite, was named Look. The other two daughters got the names Mar and Rin. They were all named one after another in the order in which they were born.

They were as pleased with their names as if they had been given the most tasty titbit.

'Your names will be famous in the realm of kingfishers if you make them so. They will be worthless if you let them be,' declared Or. 'Everything depends on you. Of course, sometimes on chance, too. But if you obey us, we shall teach you many things so that you can, my children, lead your own lives, allowing chance to interfere as little as possible in your fates. We shall tell you our own experiences, which we inherited from our fathers and mothers and gathered ourselves. Until then we shall not part; until then we shall not let you go into the world alone. Bear that in mind.'

The father and mother soon fell asleep as it was already quite late, but the young ones were still thinking about their names and could not sleep for excitement. They were very curious to know what it would ne like tomorrow when they would call one another by their new bames.

If only the night, that dreary time for sleeping, would go away — if only morning would come!

It was late when a short, piercing sound rang out in the distance and the ever-punctual echo carried it everywhere on its fast wings.

The young ones grew alarmed and jumped to their feet. The parents awoke, too.

But Father said calmly:

'Go back to sleep, nothing can happen to us. It's the voice of a rifle which man carries to hit anything that takes his fancy. He can kill a bird or an animal at a distance, even at a great distance. But he doesn't shoot at us kingfishers and other small birds. He leaves us alone.'

'He shoots at our enemies instead,' said Mother Kik, 'like magpies and jays. He likes to shoot at the hobby, too. Hobbies and eagle-owls are our greatest enemies. We're afraid of the eagle-owl more than of anything, but he can't reach into our nest, into our home.'

The young ones calmed down. Now they felt like sleep. In a moment only the sound of deep breathing could be heard from the little bundles.

Soon after they had fallen asleep a shot rang out again. But this one they slept through. Only Or heard it and, to tell the truth, he trembled.

He did not like to hear these sounds, they always terrified him. Of course, in front of the children, he could only remain calm.

Every autumn, Or and Kik would hear the shooting and see the men lining up with their guns.

The kingfishers thought that the things they carried were wooden sticks which breathed fire and smoke at one end. Too bad for any hare or any partridge, and too bad for any fox which might appear before them!

The shots carried fear and death all over the countryside.

'Shots! Shots!' Or repeated to himself, as he trembled, probably like all the other birds who had heard them. But then they were heard no more and so he stopped thinking about them, and only reminded himself again that tomorrow he had another important day.

At midnight the blackbird always awoke. He and his family were spending the night not far from the kingfishers. From time to time he gave a short, soft whistle:

'I'm up! I'm awake! I'm on the alert! I'm on guard!'

Night after night the birds heard the blackbird sentry make his announcement.

And then before morning the doe would arrive with her mate. They were Or's alarm clock.

Shsh . . .

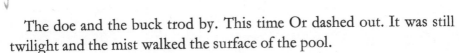

The doe and the buck trod by. This time Or dashed out. It was still twilight and the mist walked the surface of the pool.

The doe drank, and beside her the buck stood motionless staring at the opposite bank. Had he noticed something suspicious, something dangerous? Was it only a shadow, or was danger really lurking there? But then who would want to hurt these peaceful and innocent creatures? They grew a little frightened as Or suddenly waved his wings before them and uttered his morning greeting, but they immediately became quiet again. Now the buck began to drink and while he drank the doe took her turn at keeping watch. How careful and timid they were!

'I'm up, I'm up! We're going out today!' Or announced as he flew from bank to bank. He assumed that he was the first to be up and that he would wake the sleepers with his cries, but here already were the wagtail with his wife and Mr and Mrs Tit walking along the bank.

'We're going out today! Out today!' Or called to them boastfully.

Mr and Mrs Wagtail were sad. They told each other:

'Everyone is full of joy and we are full of sorrow. They are all taking out their families and our life is all in ruins. Four of our poor children have already died and the fifth one is sick.'

A chaffinch flew down on to a branch overhanging the water and sang: 'It'll rain, it'll rain!'

'The eagle-owl take you!' Or cried out at her. 'That's a nice forecast!'

'Look at the sky! Look at the sky!' she answered scornfully. 'There's going to be a downpour.'

The Blue Pool chaffinch had the reputation of being a weather prophet. Indeed, the sky was overcast with rags of cloud and the south-west wind was blowing.

'I hadn't noticed,' said Or grumpily, flying back to his nest where his children were just beginning to wake up. 'We'll put off our trip,' he told Kik. 'It's going to rain and we don't want the children to get all rumpled.'

Kik agreed, but the children insisted so much that their parents might have allowed the trip if the villagers had not appeared unexpectedly with their scythes in the meadow opposite.

It did not rain as the chaffinch had forecast, it only drizzled. The humans did not bother about this and set about scything the grass.

Immediately the wagtail arrived on the spot and asked in his agitated way, 'What are you doing here? How do you dare? Off with you!'

The humans glanced at him, smiled and paid him no further attention.

Then as the wagtail ran behind them he noticed plenty of good things to hunt in the mown grass. He quickly stopped chattering and began to pick them up.

He flew off and returned immediately with his wife. And in a while there followed blackbirds, chaffinches and goldfinches, those beautiful, timid little birds from the pine trees, looking all the time as if they had just had a surprise. And naturally the wren and his wife were among the throng.

As the villagers worked on with their sharp scythes they bared the meadow, revealing an endless supply of beetles, caterpillars and earthworms.

'We were here first,' cried the blackbirds. 'It's all ours!'

'Nonsense! Nonsense!' called the wagtails.

'Thieves! Thieves!' snapped the chaffinches as the blackbirds drove them from a cockchafer. 'Look, they want everything for themselves! Gluttons, gluttons!'

The birds might have been all on their own with no humans near.

Some of them argued at first, but they soon became sensible and settled down together to pick at the field. They had more to eat than they could consume.

Only the kingfishers did not come near the humans mowing the grass, but kept themselves to themselves by the water.

'Why not you?' asked Mr Thumb, as he carried so much food to his young ones that he bent beneath the weight.

'We can never bring ourselves to trust humans,' answered Kik. 'Never, never, never.'

'When humans are working they are nice enough. They don't bother about us. When they aren't working, it's worse; then they take notice of us.'

Mr Thumb was flying over the pool with a heavy load when he suddenly spotted a beautiful, sheeny fly. Wanting this prey, too, he opened his little beak. The larvae he was carrying fell out into the water and the fly escaped him.

'The more you have, the more you want,' laughed Kik, 'and usually you end up with nothing.'

The larvae were swallowed up by the fish as soon as they entered the water.

Father Thumb was annoyed and flew back to the meadow.

It went on drizzling for a time, but then the wind changed and the sun burst out above the forest. A seven-coloured rainbow painted itself across the distant sky.

The mowers were already a good way from the bank, so there was no need to fear them any more.

A couple of days later Or said to his wife: 'I don't want to delay the youngsters any longer, we'd better let them leave the nest.'

He waited in front of the entrance while Kik gave the news to the children, who were now more restless than ever before.

'Children, silence now, shsh,' said their mother, speaking to them seriously. 'You can go out to see the world. Your father has decided so. Of course, only for a short while. Promise that you will be quiet, as if you were in great danger and you had only your silence to hide you.'

'Ah! Ah!' the children sighed in excitement. But mother's darling exclaimed: 'Mummy, I'm frightened!'

'He's frightened!' the eldest began with a laugh, although he himself had gooseflesh all over his fisher bird's body. 'But I . . .'

'What, you? You just keep quiet,' said his mother, calling him to order. 'Have you quite forgotten what you were like? How you wept? So keep quiet, as quiet as you can. Line up by age! In front will be Father, I'll be at the back. So children, forward!'

'Mummy, Rin won't let me go first and I'm older, aren't I?' cried Mar.

'If you're naughty, you'll stay at home and you won't see anything,' said Mother calmly. 'This outing is going to be none too easy for us. When you are big, you can do whatever you choose, but now you have to obey. Do you promise?'

'We promise,' said the children, speaking with one cheep as they shuffled with little steps towards the light, on and on.

And there was Or already coming to meet them, saying to the eldest:

'When you get to the edge you must spread your wings and lightly glide down on to the ground. There's nothing to be frightened of.'

'No — I, I — I'm not — fright — frightened,' answered the eldest.

He was already right on the edge. He blinked against the bright light which seemed to be crushing him.

'On, on!' Father called from somewhere below.

The eldest one opened his eyes, spread his wings and found himself falling. He appeared in the grass beside his father without knowing how he had got there. He was very thrilled, his little heart beat fast and his little chest heaved.

'What's this, where am I lying?' he asked. But his father was already up again by the entrance to the passage calling the next fledgling, who was named after Kik, to take the plunge. Ah, how excited she was, too!

She suddenly exclaimed gaily:

'I'm flying, I'm flying! How beautiful!'

'Shsh,' hissed her father.

Then tiny Kik sank into the grass some distance from her brother because she had not folded her winglets in time.

In the end all the members of the family had flopped on to the grass and even the youngest, Look, had flown down, and not too badly either.

They were all dazzled by the brightness flooding over them and by the green and blue they saw all around.

They shrank back with fear. The fear overwhelmed their curiosity and held them to the ground. Their heads were still swimming after the flight, and they were still affected by the light. They felt gripped and squeezed by it, and they were frightened by the playful breeze which gambolled about and ran fingers through their feathers. What was it? Why did it examine them so closely?

'To me! To me!' Father called out all the time.

And, after a while, the whole brood were gathered round their parents.

'This before us is a tree,' said Or. 'Look around and see how many trees there are here. You must not hit these trees when you fly. They are just as hard as the ground, or as this stone. And that white thing you can see from here, frothing and flowing and murmuring, that is water, which gives us most of our food. Farther on the water is quieter, you'd think it was standing still. And when it is as clear as it is today, it is more than our fishing ground, it is our mirror, too — it tells us what we look like. So don't imagine, children, when you fly above the water in a few days' time that another kingfisher is flying beneath you! And now all this green and blue you can see around — that is grass and leaves of trees and bushes. And up above all this is the sky, which begins nowhere and ends nowhere. Usually it is not so blue as today.'

'What's that?' said the eldest as he pointed, terrified, at a bird swinging on a branch above them. And all except the parents quickly cringed to the ground.

'That's a siskin, he's a friend of ours,' said Kik. 'Mr Siskin, do come and look at our nest and see our family!'

'Beautiful, beautiful!' sang the siskin. 'Let me tell you, if I were to be born a second time I should want to be a kingfisher.'

'Go on with you! We can hardly get farther than our back yard and there you are wandering through the whole world. We would change places with you any day.'

'But those feathers of yours, there's splendour for you! We wander through all the world, that's true, but only because we have to. We're searching for food. If we could find it in one place like you, then we wouldn't fly away, Mrs Kingfisher. But now I must be off. And I hope that little family turns out well for you!'

'So long,' mumbled Or, who did not like chit-chat.

'How beautiful to see oneself in the mirror,' sighed little Kik. 'Am I as pretty as Mar or Rin?'

The parents laughed. 'That's my girl,' said Father Or. 'You can't hide the woman in you. And now, children, watch and see how to fly. First you jump into the air — this way.'

Or stood up on his short, strong legs. 'You throw your wings up to the sky and press them down sharply, one-two, one-two! Do you see?'

And the kingfisher flew up, higher and higher.

'Do like your father,' said Mother Kik, encouraging the children.

But at that moment Or dropped down to the bank, hissing, 'Sh! Sh! Shsh!'

On the opposite bank a man stood looking at the water. He had suddenly appeared as if out of the ground.

Or flew quickly back to his family and, cringing behind a screen of grass, they all gazed at the man.

'We're not having any luck with our outing,' said Or to Mother Kik. 'But let's hope he leaves soon.'

He was a man from the nearby village. After a while a small child came running up to him. The child jumped about and shouted and then began to chase after butterflies.

Now the man turned up his trousers and sleeves and clambered down the bank into the water. He began to catch the fish beneath the boulders with his hands. The child cried because he could not come in too. So the man threw him a shell and it kept him quiet trying to open it. But he could not manage it, for the shell was tightly closed and seemed like a stone rather than something living.

Meanwhile the man was pulling out fish, big ones and little ones, from beneath the boulders and throwing them up on to the bank. There they tossed about as they tried to find their way back into their element. Three fish, on the very edge of the bank, were successful.

'Oh! Oh!' sighed Kik.

Now the man and the child were silent, each engrossed in his work.

Up the hillside, on the doe's path, just above the kingfishers, there was a sound of crackling. And when Or looked up in surprise, he saw a hare coming down the hill.

The floppy-ears did not suspect that the man was so near, that he was running straight towards him. He had only his long ears to rely on and they heard nothing to alarm him. Before Or could let the hare know of his danger he had arrived at the water to drink.

His short-sighted eyes spotted the man only when the two-legged creature stood up and looked at him.

The hare was frightened out of his wits and scuttled back along the doe's path.

The man stopped fishing, waded to the bank and searched for the path. He found it and bent down to discover what animal used it.

At one moment he stood just beside the crouched, frightened little bundle of fisher birds and it was a wonder that he did not trample them to death.

When the man had examined the path he waded back across the pool, picked up his catch of fish from the bank, took the child into his arms and left. The terror was lifted from the kingfisher family.

'You have passed your silence test with top marks,' Or cried out delightedly. 'Yes, we were lucky,' said Kik.

Life goes on

It was quite a business getting all the family back into the nest. Puffing and straining, the young birds stretched and flapped their winglets, but when they wanted to go to the right they went to the left, and when they tried to fly to the left they ended up on the right. They did not know what to do first — to clap their wings or to steer with their tails. Having no knowledge or experience, the little birds scattered in all directions, sinking into the grass, into the ferns, into the bushes, while their parents had to flit around calling and gathering them together, telling them how to push off with their legs, how to lift themselves up and how to fly with their heads erect.

Roon almost fell into the water, while gentle little Rin got stuck on a high branch and was afraid to let go. There she was, piping and cheeping, and scared that if she flew off she would surely kill herself or end up goodness knows where and never find her way home.

Seeing her glued to the branch, whimpering away and unable to make up her mind, Mother Kik went up to encourage her and finally pushed her off. And so weeping Rin flew at last, up, then down and up again, until she hit her bill against a tree. She lurched and fell to the ground. Her bill was aching and she had black spots dancing before her eyes. She thought she would die.

But here was Father Or at her side.

'What happened to you, my darling? You're still such a little silly. There there, don't cry. Nothing's the matter, you know. You only bumped yourself a little. It'll be better in a minute. So pick yourself up like a good girl and follow your mother.'

Yes, it took some trouble and effort to pack them all back into the nest again. But at last they were all there and chattering away merrily. They had even forgotten their hunger and they were already beginning to look forward to tomorrow, to another outing.

How beautiful the world was. What magnificent pictures the light painted.

'And when you have learned to fly, we shall teach you to hunt,' their father told them.

'How wonderful that will be,' the children said. 'If only we could do it now, we can't wait.'

Or was worn out with worry. Yet he was relieved that no one had suffered any serious injury, and that no one had got lost. It had been a good day.

On the third day they had almost lost their fear of flying from the passage, and they let themselves go without protest — if only to fall like sacks of potatoes into the grass below. But now they came together again without being pushed, scurrying through the grass like little mice. And after only a week they were lining up bravely, ready to fly, rolling in the air with the aid of their tails, and competing with one another to turn corners, to cross the pool and to stay longest off the ground.

They had a gay time. They frolicked, teased, spurred one another on to greater and greater feats.

And they already knew, too, most of the inhabitants of the pool, and would greet them when they met them and would politely answer their inquiries about how their parents were and how all the family were getting on. Apart from the wagtails, the neighbours they liked most of all were Mr Thumb, that bright and friendly twitterer, and his family. The young wrens, too, had now left their nest to frolic about under the eyes of their parents.

The wagtail, of course, had no time to hang about chatting. No sooner had he stopped for a moment than he was scurrying along, flying off again to hunt for food for his young cuckoo who had now kicked his last child out of the nest. The poor little thing was lying now on the hard ground beside the nest, cheeping with hunger. He might have perished like his brothers and sisters. But he did not. His parents managed to nourish him and by good luck nothing came to snatch him up.

The little kingfishers were curious to see that strange and ever-hungry young bird who had been hatched in the wagtail nest.

Led by the eldest, they called on the wagtails and saw the great ugly thing. When the young cuckoo saw them he opened his beak, flapped his wings and screeched so strangely that the little fisher birds grew terrified and flew straight off.

Day quickly followed day and the kingfishers soon learned to hunt. They were keen enough, but they did not relish the sitting and waiting. They tried to catch the fish which came to the shallow to bask in the sun or look for something tasty to eat.

'You will be feeding yourselves soon, and that will take a load off our minds,' said Mother Kik.

'Surely they're big and clever enough already,' said Father, boosting their self-confidence and pride. 'Even Rin can glide and dart like a real kingfisher girl now.'

'Yes,' Rin said. 'I caught three dragonflies and could have caught five if brother Or hadn't taken two right out of my bill.'

'Could, could! What are you saying?' said Father. 'Of course you couldn't when your brother was faster than you. And next time don't tell tales and don't complain.'

'And I caught two flies and found one slug,' boasted young Kik. 'It's called a slug, that thing without any legs, isn't it?'

'And I, I — I caught an enormous beetle! I had to fight him,' cried the youngest, Look. 'It was a tough fight, but I beat him. Daddy said it was a great water beetle.'

'Yes, yes,' said his mother, smiling. 'How quickly you pick things up. I'm very glad. There's no one like you, you little bragger.'

Night was falling. Today they had stayed out rather later than usual and suddenly they heard above them a gruesome noise: 'Hoo-hoo, oo-hoo, oo-hoo.'

'Oh, horror! Horror, children! It's the eagle-owl,' wailed Kik.

'Quiet! Sh!' whispered Or. 'Down behind me! Quiet, quiet or we're done for!'

'Hoo-oohoo!' came the sound again, this time from somewhere quite near to the kingfishers.

'Quickly, under here!' ordered Or.

They were a few steps from a grey boulder overgrown with moss. With a flash they were under it, out of breath and with their hearts beating fast. They pressed against one another in a small bundle.

Wasn't someone missing? Yes, Look.

'Where has he got to, poor child?' his mother sobbed quietly. 'I must go and look for him.'

Or could hardly hold her back and they all had to pin her down with their bills. If she had slipped out, the eagle-owl would certainly have got her.

The kingfishers were even more alarmed when the bird of prey settled right on top of their boulder.

The eagle-owl mumbled to himself for a while, and then they heard the whirr of his great wings.

Had he flown away or not? The flight of nocturnal birds of prey is so quiet that you cannot hear them until it is too late, until a terrible beak has grasped you and sharp, pitiless talons have fixed into your flesh.

'Where's Look? Where's Look?' wept Kik.

'He's sure to be safe,' said Or, trying to comfort his wife. 'He's clever enough to know that when there's danger, he must be as still and silent as a stone.'

They whispered together, their words sounding like the breathing of a gentle wind.

'Hoo-hoo-oohoo!' came an echo from somewhere on the other side of the pool.

Or immediately darted out.

'Up! Up!' he called. 'And straight home, home, home!'

'Look!' they all cried at the top of their voices. And then Look appeared.

He joined the rest of the family, all clamouring to get into the passage. 'Slowly, one after another!' cried Or. 'If you all try to get in at once, you'll only start fighting and then none of you will get in. Remember that! . . . And where have you been, Look?'

'I ran after you, but I was caught in the grass and got left behind,' said Look. 'So I pressed to the ground beneath the leaves of a fern. I saw the enemy settle right on the boulder you were hiding under. He just sat there and waited. He looked around — such yellow eyes he had, they made me feel sick! Oh, what a terrible time I had! I thought you didn't know he was there and that you would go to look for me. Then he flew away and began to hoot when he thought there was no one about. Oh, why are there such nasty birds in the world, Mummy? Why don't they leave us alone? What have we done to them that they want to catch us?'

'I don't know,' said his mother. 'But big birds like him aren't our only enemies, you realize. There are also animals like weasels and rats, and squirrels, who like to find birds' eggs and make a meal of them.'

And Father added:

'Everyone eats what he has to. Owls catch birds and mice and we for our part go after dragonflies, beetles and fish. We can't do otherwise. If we could feed on plants as the doe does we wouldn't hunt for prey and we would have an easier living. But we need something that has drawn breath, indeed we are birds of prey, just like eagle-owls, except that we don't fancy killing other birds. Apart from beetles, flies and dragonflies, we catch only fish. It's a nasty habit, a real crime, to make a meal of a bird. We kingfishers will never reduce ourselves to that. Death to owls!'

Or hardly slept that night, he spent nearly the whole time on guard listening to the hooting of the eagle-owl. Now here, now there, echoed his artful, cruel call.

'Oohoo, I'm king of the forest!'

'Fortunately,' Or told his children next morning when they asked him whether they could go out, 'fortunately, owls can see only very badly in the day; in the daylight they are as good as blind and they are afraid to fly. They can't see in the sunlight, just as we can't see in the dark.' And then he added: 'Today, children, we must go to bed early.'

'Yes, it's always a bad time when an eagle-owl moves in,' said Kik. 'We can never feel safe when he's about. I wish to goodness someone would break his neck for him.'

'If only a human would take him,' cheeped the cuddlesome Look, who had had the biggest fright of all.

The battle

When the kingfisher family flew out above the Blue Pool they heard the news.

The wagtail's odd child had been devoured by the eagle-owl. While that terrible bird had been roving about he had knocked a wing against the tree above the wagtail's nest. The unfortunate young cuckoo had begun to cry, assuming that one of his foster-parents was bringing him food.

At once the eagle-owl had fallen upon him and gobbled him up.

You might have thought that the wagtails would have been glad, but they paraded up and down loudly lamenting:

'Poor child, poor little fellow!'

They had already become accustomed to him and had even grown to like him. This was in spite of the fact that after growing big and strong so quickly the cuckoo had destroyed their other children by pushing them out of their own nest.

'There's still time, you can still begin a new nest,' said Mr Thumb, trying to comfort them in their loss.

'The children would never grow up now before the winter,' the wagtail answered sadly. 'Unfortunately, it's too late for us.'

'Yes, yes, we shall feel sad when we go south this year,' added Mrs Wagtail. 'We always flew there with a full brood before.'

'You should build your home in a different way, my friends,' the kingfisher told them. 'I'll always go on telling you the same thing. You may be clever, perhaps the cleverest of us all, but you don't live in a clever way. You ought to live as we do.'

'What's the good of telling us that when we can't help doing things our own way?' replied Mr Wagtail.

'No, no, I wouldn't live under the ground for anything in the world,' added Mrs Wagtail. 'When I sit on my nest I must see what's going on around me all the time. I would feel buried, under the ground.'

'Well,' said Kik, 'if you won't take advice . . .'

'Come on, Kik, what good is advice if we can't follow it? And what about you? You spend the winter here and we don't. Why don't you fly away for the winter? Every time we migrate to warmer places, I say to the kingfishers: "Leave here and fly with us." But they just shake their heads and say: "We can't, we can't keep flying for so long." '

'True, true,' said Mr Thumb, nodding his head, 'one bird's meat is another bird's poison. I shouldn't like to fly away either. We've managed here before and we'll manage again. We'll always get through the winter somehow. If only we didn't have this vermin, this eagle-owl who never lets us feel safe in the night.'

The children of the wren and the kingfisher listened wide-eyed to these words, glancing furtively up at the sky as if something horrible were hanging there about to fall upon them.

Now they heard a rustling — their eyes fixed on the old alder and they saw a big grey ball of feathers. What could it be?

And Look cried out in terror:

'There he is! There's the murderer! He was listening to us! Let's flee, he'll be after us and eat us all!'

'What's up? What's up? What's up?' asked the blackbird, who was picking wild strawberries nearby. 'What's up, children?'

'Where? Where? Where? What is it?' the wagtail cried out in alarm.

'There! There! There!' called Look, pointing to the tree and trembling all over.

Indeed, the eagle-owl was sleeping in the alder where he had found such a tasty prey.

'I'll pick his eyes out!' cried the wagtail.

'Let's chase him off so fast that he won't feel like coming back,' all the birds cried.

There were more of them all the time, flying in from every direction, and they all attacked the eagle-owl.

The blackbird was the boldest, but neither the thrushes nor the kingfishers held back.

'Come on, everyone, after the intruder! Let's kill him, or he'll kill us! Come on, come on, everyone, our lives are all at stake!' the wagtail kept on calling out.

The eagle-owl crouched helplessly, furiously blinking his yellow eyes. From time to time he braced himself to lunge with his beak or flap his wings.

The birds attacked the villain with growing fury and violence just as they had attacked the cuckoo before. The owl defended himself like a blind man or like someone who has been attacked on a dark night.

But the small, short beaks did not hurt him. Some of his feathers flew, of course, but what did that matter?

The cry and roar reached the ears of the crows, who used to search the banks of the brook every morning. When they saw that it was not the cuckoo under attack, but the murderer of their own fellow crows and the robber of their nests, they came to the aid of the Blue Pool defenders.

Powerful black wings whirred above the fighting, and the eagle-owl knew that if he was not enjoying himself now, he would soon be in real trouble.

'It's you who killed our old leader last year,' the first crow called out.

'It's you who plundered our nests on the old pine tree,' cried the second.

'You cowards!' the eagle-owl shouted at them. 'Do you really want to fight a blind bird? If you have a bit of honour you'll wait for dusk!'

What honour has he? He attacks in the night when we can't see, thought the birds of the Blue Pool as they drew back, so as not to be swept away or crushed in the real battle which was now beginning.

The crows launched a joint attack from all sides. They were five, and a sixth was gliding in.

But the eagle-owl, who was used to tough fights, lifted himself up in all his strength, flapped his wings and lunged with his fearful beak to ward off the pitiless attackers.

Only now did the real hue and cry begin.

The noise of the battle echoed far and wide and the youngsters of the Blue Pool fled and hid. Only the old birds dared to stay to see what would happen.

'Caw! Caw! Caw! Call yourself a king, you great ugly thing?' cried the oldest of the five black avengers as he struck the eagle-owl a heavy blow between the eyes with his wing. At that moment there was a single dense throng of crows and the eagle-owl. A single, madly twisting, tossing mass fell to the ground and rolled about, groaning and crying and screeching.

One crow, struck on the head by the eagle-owl, lay motionless on the ground. Another had a broken leg.

The eagle-owl bravely shook off the attackers and it already seemed that he would be the victor. The three remaining crows flew away bleeding, while the old killer bird of the forest stood up again on his strong and fearful talons.

'Now we're done for!' cried the birds of the Blue Pool.

'Hahaa!' laughed the eagle-owl, his blind yellow eyes shining cruelly.

But then the crow with the broken leg rose up and flew off for reinforcements. In a while he was back with new black warriors.

The eagle-owl pressed himself against the old hollow trunk, covering his back. He had a good position for the ensuing fight.

The crow reinforcements did not yet dare to attack.

'You've struck me lame,' the crow with the broken leg cried out. 'You've crippled me for life! I won't give up until you are defeated. You have crippled me and killed my friend. I won't give up until I've called all the crows to destroy you!'

'Hahaa,' replied the eagle-owl mockingly, 'just any of you dare to come near; I'll stand up to all your cowardly breed, hahaa! I'll hold out until evening and then I'll have you, I shan't spare a soul!'

And then something extraordinary happened.
From the depth of the forest a human emerged
with a gun over his shoulder. He stopped and
listened quietly to the crows' abuse and the eagle-
owl's bold laugh.

At that moment the crows became silent
and with the speed of lightning they fell
away — they had caught sight of the human
and fled.

'Hahaa!' laughed the eagle-owl, who had not
seen the real reason for the crows' retreat.
'Have you lost your courage, then? Have you fled,
you cowards?'

After a while he, too, suspected that something
strange was happening. He grew silent and
bristled up.

He caught the scent of a human body.

The human put his gun aside — and the birds
of the Blue Pool, hidden behind the leaves, saw him
draw near to the eagle-owl. Unable to see his enemy,
the bird of prey lashed out with a wing, jabbed
with his beak and was just about to fly off. It was
too late.

The human caught him in his strong arms
by the head and legs, thrust him face downwards
on to the ground, knelt on him and bound his
legs and wings so that he could not move.
Now he held him up, looked at him and
smiled at his helplessness.

It was the gamekeeper.

He picked up his gun and carried the eagle-
owl into captivity.

He had been wandering about the forest
and had come down to the path by the pool,
hurrying there when he had heard the
wild cry of battle. He was glad to have caught

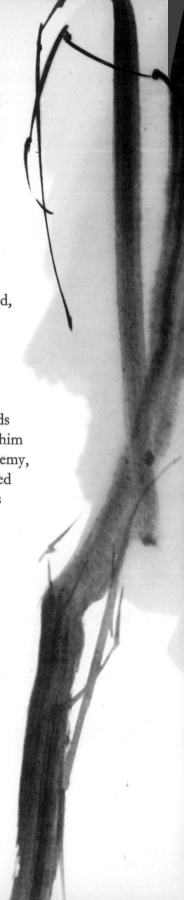

the bird of prey so easily after having searched for it for so long. It had played havoc with the young partridges and hares and, as the law of life bids, had throttled everything that it had found alive in the night.

The eagle-owl had almost cleared his own territory of birds. That was why the great plunderer had turned to the Blue Pool, which he had found rich with prey.

He was the last of his breed in those parts. For many a mile all the eagle-owls had been exterminated, but he alone had survived and escaped the gamekeeper's attention, thanks only to his unusual caution and cunning.

The nocturnal bird of prey had lived high up in an ancient oak, where no one except a few black woodpeckers had known about him. But when they had seen him during their search for larvae and beetles, they had quickly fled and not ventured into his tree again.

The eagle-owl's great days of hunting had now come to an end.

The gamekeeper took him home, brought down a large cage with strong bars and put the eagle-owl inside it. The eagle-owl beat furiously against the bars, sure that he could break them and escape from his prison. It was in vain. The bars of the cage did not give way, and the eagle-owl only stained himself with blood.

The gamekeeper's children came and threw him meat. He was hungry and it smelt good but, hurt by his defeat and loss of freedom, he would not even touch it.

I will die, I will die of hunger rather than lead such a miserable life, the old hunter of the forest said to himself.

But during the night he changed his mind. For hunger is stronger than many a good resolution.

He began to eat and after a while he became used to the cage, too.

The man succeeded in taming him even to eat from his hand. The eagle-owl became dull and stupid, like anyone who has lost his freedom for a long time, like any slave.

Summer
is ending

The birds of the Blue Pool rejoiced that the menace had been carried off and would never return.

The dead crow still lay on the path where the famous combat had taken place. Who would remove him? He lay there, a haunting sight. No one wished to touch him, no one wished even to look at the black warrior who had given his life for the freedom and happiness of the birds living around the pool.

And so when the birds were sickened by the sight of his body, the ants began to pay attention to it. They gathered from far and wide in the forest — who can tell how they had heard about the crow? — and picked at the particles of skin and flesh, clearing the body so thoroughly that in two weeks there was nothing but bones left under the stiff, black feathers. Then when a heavy rainstorm came it soaked and loosened the clumps of feathers and the wind blew them away.

Summer was leaving the hillside. The days sank one after another beyond the pool into eternity.

All the fledglings hatched this year now looked just like their parents and, of course, they were earning their own livings, too.

Many of the young ones had flown off to different parts, and were living on their own. Only the kingfishers kept together under the eyes of Or and Kik.

They were still learning to hunt, and they still did not know all they had to. A kingfisher's life is a hard one and so it takes fisher birds longer to learn. Those birds who earned their livings easily knew everything by now: how to pick raspberries, catch beetles, clear twigs of greenflies or seize caterpillars. But great sharpness, skill and patience are demanded of the young kingfishers for their hunting.

First of all, kingfishers must find a remote place with shallow water where the sun can shine and show up the fish. They have to know how to fly with their wings and steer with their tails. And above all they have to know how to dive, holding their breath, falling into the water like stones and swimming swiftly out again! Summer is no problem, it is good to be alive then. But in autumn, about November, that is when trouble starts. The water gets muddy and the beetles hide away so that you would need to look under the turf to get them. And as for winter — well, we have already experienced that with the kingfishers.

The kingfishers were still sleeping together in the old tunnel, their hard-won home, but now if one of the family stayed out overnight, Kik was no longer worried, knowing that she would see him again the next day.

As the pool was now nearly empty of fish, the young fisher birds set out upstream with their father to discover new bends of the brook, new pools, new territories. But where the chances for hunting were best, other kingfishers were already living and jealously protecting their domains.

'Off with you, off with you!' they cried at Or and Kik and their family as they flew out to defend their hunting grounds.

Every hillside, every corner of the forest, every meadow rang and bubbled with life.

Then the leaves began to turn yellow as the sun rose later each day.

In the meadow opposite the Blue Pool the second crop of hay was being gathered. And again one of the mowers, just as he had earlier in the spring, stopped work and went to the brook to fish. And, as before, the doe and buck went down to drink, too. When they spotted the man they immediately turned and bounded back into the forest darkness. They thought that the man had not noticed them, but they were mistaken.

Again the human waded across the brook and again he traced the path with his mysterious eyes. He distinguished the impressions of hooves and gave a smile — just as he had in the spring.

The next night Or in his tunnel caught the sound of suspicious steps outside.

No, these were not the steps of the buck or doe!

Who was it? What did he want? Was it danger again drawing near? Hadn't there been enough danger already?

There was a whisper. It sounded like the wind rustling the trees, the crowns of the young oaks. Then everything was silent. Or tried in vain to guess what it could be. In the end, sleep closed his eyes.

He may not have been asleep for long when he was awoken by a frantic stamping and the sound of groans more painful than any he had heard for many a day. He woke his family and darted out.

It was not yet daylight. In the early dawn the buck could be seen rising on his hind legs. Now he fell back on all fours, but some mysterious, evil power lifted him up, again and again. Beside him stood the doe, who saw what was happening to her husband, but could not understand it. The buck was being pulled up by a wire tied round a young oak. He tried to free himself, but with each violent movement the snare grew tighter. Who had set it?

The doe stood helpless by the buck, looking round in alarm and then turning back again to her trapped mate.

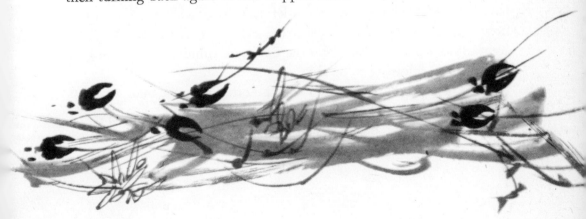

What was the matter with him? What had happened to him?

The buck had been trapped by a poacher's noose which the human had set — he had bent the young oak down to the ground and tied it with the noose to the grass, so lightly that the slightest touch would release it.

The buck had put his head through the snare without noticing it. Immediately the oak had straightened and the noose had pulled on his neck and dragged him up. The buck stood there now on his hind legs, jerking his body helplessly.

'Oh, my buck! My buck!' the doe called to him. 'What are you doing? What has happened to you? Oh! Oh!'

She wanted to help him, but she did not know how to. She butted him in her despair.

The buck's whole body swung against the tree — and suddenly he dropped to the ground as the wire broke and the snare loosened.

The buck lay motionless in the undergrowth, perhaps already dead. The doe licked him and he began to get back his breath. Yes, he was breathing. After a moment he raised his head and tried to stand up. He could hardly keep his feet. But he was alive, and that was the main thing!

'What was the matter with you?' asked the doe.

He could not answer yet. They heard the rustle of branches, the whisper of grass and the sound of steps, human steps.

The human was coming.

The buck had just enough strength to stagger into the thicket and to run off with the doe. They ran faster and faster.

When the human reached the oak, he cursed, as he saw that his work with the noose had been in vain. In his imagination he had already loaded the roebuck on to his shoulder and carried it secretly home. But now he could not find even his snare. He swore as he left. While he went off in anger, the buck and the doe were running in another part of the forest, rejoicing to be alive.

Or recognized the human. It was none other than the man who had left the haymaking to go and fish in the Blue Pool.

From that time no one saw the roebuck any more. They ran in other places, far from there.

Good luck!

'Summer's on the wane, summer's on the wane,' sang Mr Wagtail. And Mrs Wagtail agreed. 'Time to fly, time to fly,' cried out Mr Wagtail. And Mrs Wagtail added: 'Fly to the sun, to the sun.'

And so sang other birds, too.

The stock-doves, those shy and mistrustful creatures, were already gone.

It was quite a sight in the summer to see them returning with their families in the evening to their native spruces above the pool after pasturing on the distant fields. Their wings shone in the setting sun — they were splendid flyers, those stock-doves, they could escape even the goshawks.

Some families had already flown away at about the end of August.

'They can't complain,' Mr Wagtail would say to Mr Thumb. 'In a day they get I don't know how far, they fly over hill and dale, while we have to drag ourselves along the brooks and rivers, half on the wing, half on foot. You should try it some time and fly with us, wren.'

'Not me! Not me!' answered Mr Wren. 'I don't feel the cold and I can always manage to get by, even when it snows. I'm a humble chap, I don't need much for a living.'

'Summer's on the wane, summer's on the wane,' Mr and Mrs Wagtail went on singing. They were free now and only seldom did they remember their giant foster-child, who had been swallowed by the eagle-owl in the spring.

The cuckoo's second young one had died, too. He had grown very hungry inside the hollow alder — the hole was too small for him to get out and the titmice could not support him any longer; it was beyond their strength.

The young cuckoo would not stop crying:

'I'm hungry! I'm hungry!'

His sorrowful voice grew weaker and weaker until it became silent for ever.

His grey-plumed mother used to fly to him, but she did not know how to feed him. She wanted to take him with her, but her efforts came to nothing. Of course, she had other children in various places so she hurried to them. Most of them, unfortunately, did not turn out well.

'Summer's on the wane, summer's on the wane,' sang the wagtail. 'Time to fly, time to fly,' added Mrs Wagtail. 'To the south, to the south.'

In the morning and in the evening the mist fell over the Blue Pool. In the morning it veiled the sun, in the evening it hid the stars.

One morning, in the mist, and it was perhaps even before the break of day, a great whirr of wings sounded above the pool. A large crowd of storks landed. And those normally taciturn birds began to talk and talk, they cried out and argued like an agitated crowd of humans. They walked about the meadow, waded in the pool, flew up in the air and then came down again by the water's edge.

The inhabitants of the Blue Pool who still remained — many families had already left — were all put out by this conference of storks.

The kingfishers withdrew into their tunnel and did not dare to show their heads.

Of course, Father Or stayed on guard by the entrance.

But the storks did not hurt anybody, they merely argued all the while among themselves and it was a long time before they grew silent. Then they left as calmly as they had arrived.

They flew off slowly and seemed to be rowing in the air. They flew one behind another and only then, above the forest, did they line up and form a V with the strongest and most experienced stork at the head. They flew away to the south.

The wagtails followed soon after.

'See you next year,' cried Mr Wagtail.

'Keep well,' Mrs Wagtail wished them.

'Have a good journey and a safe return,' called the kingfishers and the wrens.

'It's a pity they have to go,' said Mrs Chaffinch, 'we'd got so used to them. They were certainly good neighbours.'

'Yes, and think how well they guarded our pool,' said Or. To which Kik nodded her head approvingly.

'Well, they'll come back safe and sound, don't worry,' twittered Mr Wren, disappearing into the bushes, which were now half bare.

'But why do some birds have to go away?' the young kingfishers asked their parents. 'Why do they have to go, and not we? Why do they have to fly away to other places somewhere in the south?'

'All these neighbours of ours who fly away, who fly away to the south where it is warm,' answered Or, 'could never feed themselves here in the winter. They fly away to save their lives. Mostly they feed on insects and in the autumn and winter the insects here are hiding under the grass, or in the ground or beneath the bark of trees.'

'The swallows told me that insects burrow into the crevices of houses, too,' said Kik.

'But mostly they die, they have only short lives,' concluded Father Or.

'How could the swallows, those beautiful things, possibly live here in winter,' said Kik smiling, 'when there are no flies to eat?'

'Are they prettier than we are?' asked Rin.

'You are beautiful in your own way,' Mrs Thumb, who happened to be around, said spitefully. 'But aren't my children the prettiest of all at the Blue Pool?'

'I like the wild duck,' said young Or. 'They are nearly as pretty as we are. But when they feed on fish like us, why do they fly away and we don't?'

'Simply because we don't feel like going away anywhere,' said his father grumpily. 'Just as the wrens and the titmice don't.'

The chaffinches flew in as he finished speaking.

'We don't feel like going either, we don't, we don't,' sang Mr Chaffinch.

'What do we lack?' asked his wife. 'And when the winter grows too hard, we'll go into the villages and there we shall always earn a living along with the sparrows and chickens. We don't feel like leaving, we don't, we don't,' she sang softly. 'We like it here all the time, we do, we do.'

The leaves were falling fast, the winds were growing colder and more violent and the rains were setting in. But there was still food enough and to spare. And when the stomach is full even foul weather is easily borne. The fish were fat and lazy, they were easy to catch. There were plenty of snails lying about in the shallow water and many dying beetles gathered on branches and under banks of leaves.

The children were now so skilful at everything that you could hardly distinguish them from the old ones. They now knew nearly all they needed for life.

So let winter come!

And winter was, of course, not long in coming. One morning they awoke to see everything looking grey and white. The world was covered with hoar-frost.

'What's happened?' asked the puzzled children.

'Winter's here, winter's here,' called their father. 'And it will be better for us than all that rain which only made the water muddy. But later on, when the pool's frozen, it will be worse. Things could get very bad indeed. It would be a good idea, children, if you began to look now for your own hunting grounds so that you have a better chance of catching fish. We're too many in one place here.'

Kik only sighed and no one felt very gay.

They could all see that the time for parting was not far off.

The days were growing shorter all the time. But after the hoar-frost and after the first sharp frost of winter the weather warmed up and it seemed that life would be easy again.

But the rain set in and a furious gale blew. The water became muddy and the level rose high. Fallen leaves and branches were carried down the fast-flowing stream and nests hung from the trees like scraps of grass.

Where were the birds who had lived in them? Who could tell?

Only now did the young kingfishers feel what it was like to be hungry, what it was like to fly and fly, searching for food in vain.

They still flew together, but soon they set out separately for remote places, and only in the evening did they gather again on their old nest.

In the morning and early in the evening, mists flooded the valley and the kingfishers were all bedraggled when they came together at night.

From time to time the sun still found some strength and dispersed the mists. Days full of glitter still returned and the water became clean and the fishing was rich.

Suddenly one night the snow fell. It mostly melted during the day. The sun turned red before setting, the red sky shone through the forest like a distant fire, like blood — it promised frost, and that night the frost struck, covering all the water with ice.

After that the sun did not appear again for several days. The frost grew sharper and then relaxed a little, and the snow began to fall heavily. And it fell and fell until the trees and bushes and the whole pool were hidden, and the whole world was white.

It was then that the kingfishers missed their eldest child, young Or. He appeared after several days to find the rest of the family starving.

'So there you are!' he called, seeing the family. 'How are you getting on?'

'Badly!' his mother burst out. 'This is the worst time of all for our breed!'

'You must come with me, then. I haven't much to offer you, but you may find it will do for a modest living. '

Young Or had settled in the mill where his father and mother had

once spent the night. He
had made his home by the big wheel
in the room which the miller called the
wheel-house.

The water flowed into the wheel-house
from the mill-race and fell on to the
water-wheel, making it turn. The wheel
turned and set the mill course moving
in the grinding room. There the grain
was ground into flour.

Even if the mill-race was frozen
the water still flowed under the
ice just as it does in a river or brook.
It carried fish into the wheel-house
where they fell from the wheel and
either stayed on the floor or flowed
out along the mill-race and back into
the brook.

The kingfisher family settled down
on the beams and ledges inside the
wheel-house. With the speed of lightning they flew down to snap up the
fish which the wheel cast off.

Besides humans, there were dogs
and cats living at the mill. The dogs
did not bother them, but the cats often
looked into the wheel-house. They
would have liked to have had a go
at the kingfishers, but they could
not stay long as they felt the cold.
So they softly padded away.

The miller had a grown-up
daughter and two boys who were still
at school. Sometimes they all came
into the wheel-house.

'They're beautiful, aren't they?' said

the girl to the boys. 'It's good that they live here. Just as swallows bring happiness to the house where they nest, so kingfishers bring happiness to the mill where they stay. You must never hurt them. Nor any song-birds either.'

'That's why we've made a birdhouse, as we learned at school, Rosie,' said the elder boy, 'and because we like them, too, and don't want them to go hungry in the winter.'

'But kingfishers aren't song-birds, are they?' said the younger boy.

'I know that, silly,' answered Rosie. 'They may not be much good as singers, but they are such beautiful birds, and when the sun shines they look like gems flying through the air.'

While outside the winds blew, the snow fell and the frost held everything in its grip, here in the wheel-house it was like a cosy nook.

Though the kingfishers were doing well and they had nothing much to complain about, still they did not enjoy the long time of winter. Winter, who can be fond of winter?

'Winter, go away!' Father Or would call. 'Do go away!'

The nights were long to live through. And yet they grew shorter, the sun grew white, and soon it began to smile and be warm.

'It's coming at last!' said Mother Kik, smiling.

The kingfishers started flying out again. And the snow crept away.

The snow slipped first from the southern hillsides and tiny white flowers appeared beneath the black, stretching bushes. And on the tip of the tallest spruce, standing guard over the valley, a blackbird was tuning up like someone trying an instrument that had been put away for a long time: yes, yes, it would be all right, the bird as black as jet with the yellow bill would whistle gaily again.

That night the ice cracked, broke up and began to leave. The young kingfishers grew frightened, but their parents were happy to hear the crunching noise.

Then came the day with a bright, white sun and the birds flew out from the water-mill together. Beautiful fisher birds of blue, red and yellow!

It was Sunday; the miller's daughter, Rosie, had just come out of the house in her Sunday best and was hurrying to the town to meet her young man.

'Look,' she called back to her mother indoors, 'our kingfishers! How beautiful, how wonderful!'

Was it not that same Rosie who, in the spring, had persuaded the stubborn boy to put the helpless little bird back into his nest? Little did she know that one of the sturdy young kingfishers now dazzling her eyes was the baby Or she had saved.

The kingfishers flew by in a flash and settled some distance away on the roots of an old alder by the droning brook. Below its roots on the wet, sandy bank, splinters of ice thrown up by the water glittered like silver in the sunbeams.

And just then Father Or said:

'We got through the winter very well. For that we can thank our eldest. The main thing is that none of us lost his life or even got hurt. So many kingfishers do lose their lives in winter. We were lucky that we could stay together. But now the time for farewells has come. In fact we should have parted long ago.'

'Yes, we should long ago,' said Mother Kik. 'But I'm glad it happened this way.'

'When should we have parted?' asked the ever-curious Rin.

'Way back in the autumn, once you had learned to fly and to earn your own living,' replied Mother Kik.

'Your mother and I shall return to our old hunting ground,' said Father Or.

'To the Blue Pool,' added his wife.

'And each of you, children, must now look for a new home of your own,' said Or, nodding his head seriously.

'But first you must find husbands and wives,' said Mother Kik. 'Otherwise you could not found your families. And without a family and children, life would have no sense, we would live and die in vain, like apple trees without fruit.'

'And remember that your home will be a happy one only if you are ready to face danger,' spoke Father Or. 'Don't be cowards, don't be frightened to defend yourselves against any enemy.'

'Your father is right, children,' said Mother Kik. And droplets of tears rolled down the side of her neck. She was crying as every mother does when she parts with her children.

'Farewell! Farewell!' the children called as they flapped their wings before flying off.

The young kingfishers, all handsome boys and girls, flew off in a bunch and their parents watched them rising, scattering, gaily dodging here and there and coming together again.

And then they saw them above the last bend of the brook suddenly disperse: in a second they had disappeared from sight.

Farewell! Good luck! See you again!

Author's note

When I was a boy, I used to walk to school, more than an hour's journey from my home. For most of the way I followed a footpath along a brook running through the forest. The brook was full of fish, and the forest and fields were full of birds and animals. Since that time, I have been fond of nature, of the trees, rocks, water, fields and all their inhabitants.

We lived in a lonely house and for more than three years I went to school by myself. And so it was quite natural that I should see the life along my path more sharply than my friends who lived in the town.

Of all the birds, I liked the kingfisher best. I used to see it fishing in the mill-pond.

Perhaps you know that gorgeous bird?

It is very shy. It just flashes past you like a shiny blue and red arrow and it is gone. You need great patience to discover its way of life and, above all, where it nests.

Once, you could have met it on every brook, not to mention every river, and on almost every pond and lake. In recent decades kingfishers have dwindled greatly in number. They have fled from those waters where man has spread his works. That is understandable. But what makes the kingfisher desert even those places as yet untouched by human schemes?

I have often recalled that daily journey of mine. Indeed, who does not recall the time of his childhood, when golden gates open and we begin to see and discover and know the world in which we live?

Often in memory I talked with that lost world, until one day I felt an urgent need to write about the life of the mill-pond in the forest; about that blue pool, above all about the kingfishers, those feathered fishermen, and of course about their friends and acquaintances, too. I wanted so much to introduce readers to the joys and sorrows of our fellow creatures.

How should I do it?

When as a boy I saw the birds and animals by the water and in the forests and fields, I always felt sorry that none of them could speak a language that we might understand. Neither a kingfisher nor a wagtail, neither a doe nor a horse can tell us anything. A song-bird sings, a frog croaks, a dog barks. They do not speak. And yet, if we become familiar with the lives of birds and animals, we see that they can make themselves understood one to another by voice and movement.

A song-bird sings in one way when it feels well and gay, in another when it sees danger for itself and its companions: then it sounds an alarm which a doe or a fox can understand, too.

'Watch out, a cat's prowling about! Watch out, a human is coming!'

When I was a boy, as I have told you, I would have been very glad if nature had spoken in human language, and all of nature! Even an ancient pine, not only the creatures living in it. In fairy-tales, which used to make my eyes grow wide with wonder and excitement, all things behave like living creatures endowed with speech: a pigeon or a stag can speak, just the same as a cloud, just the same as a woodman or a peasant.

'And so he asked the silver birch and the birch said to him . . .' — 'And so he asked the spring and the spring began to speak . . .'

We children understood very well, even though we knew that neither a silver birch nor a spring could ever utter a single word, apart from the rustle of its leaves or the murmur of its water.

And so I knew now how to depict the life of the kingfisher, as well as the lives and adventures of the other birds and all the activity of the pool of water in the middle of the forest, of the mill-pond which I called the Blue Pool.

I tried to choose the simplest form and the simplest words. That is not so easy as it might seem.

The small boy, who lived for so long in friendship with the world of the brook and the forest, had his beautiful dream come true only many years later. 'His' birds speak now among themselves and about themselves!

I wrote the story out of my love of nature and from a wish to share at least a part of this love with all who read this book.